DEAD MAN'S
CREEK

Also by Lee Martin

Shadow on the Mesa
Fast Ride to Boot Hill
The Last Wild Ride
The Grant Conspiracy: Wake of the Civil War
Fury at Cross Creek
In Mysterious Ways
Revenge at Rawhide
The Maverick Gun
Fury at Sweetwater Pass
The Lone Rider
Black River
Dead Man's Trail
Valley of the Lawless
Track the Men Down
The Danger Trail
Hang Town

The Darringer Brothers Series:

Trail of the Fast Gun
Trail of the Long Riders
Trail of the Hunter
Trail of the Circle Star
Trail of the Restless Gun
Trail of the Dangerous Gun

and coming soon...
Ride the Wild Wind

DEAD MAN'S CREEK

Lee Martin

Vaca Mountain Press
Vacaville, California, USA

Vaca Mountain Press
Paperback ISBN 13: 978-1-952380-58-7
Kindle ISBN 13: 978-1-952380-59-4

Also available in
Large Print ISBN 13: 978-1-952380-60-0

Cover design by Christopher Wait, High Pines Creative, for ENC Graphic Services
Cover photograph © Getty Images
Interior design by Deirdre Wait, High Pines Creative, for ENC Graphic Services

Published by Vaca Mountain Press
Vacaville, California, U.S.A.

Visit Lee Martin Westerns on Facebook.

To my wonderful family
and in loving memory of my beautiful
sister and best friend Arlene,
and of our blessed mother,
our rough riding brothers,
and of Jim Liontas.

DEAD MAN'S CREEK

CHAPTER ONE

C olby Dancer was his name, and every man in New Mexico Territory gave him plenty of room. But on an evening in May of 1877, as he rode back into the town of Slye, west of Lincoln, a rustler's body over a trailing saddle horse, everyone dove for cover.

The elderly town marshal peered out the window of his office, his mustache twitching, as his young, pink-faced deputy crowded his elbow. They were squinting in the glare of the setting sun and watching Colby approach.

"What you gonna do when you tell him, marshal?"

"Run like blazes."

"Why's everybody so scared of him, anyhow?"

"He hunts rustlers for Chisum."

"I know that, but everybody's hidin', afraid of what he's gonna do now. But he never looked that tough to me. Oh, sure he's big, but so what?"

"He's a man who doesn't drink hard liquor, and he don't chew or smoke, and I hardly ever heard him cuss. Even when his girl ran off with a peddler, he didn't crack."

"Maybe that's why she ran off," the deputy said.

"If he has to kill a rustler, you can't even tell if it bothers him. But when he finds out what happened now, he's going to explode, and he's got no natural way to do that. If I was you, I'd leave."

The deputy straightened, drawing himself up tall. "I ain't scared of nobody. Besides, anybody that weird has got to have scrambled eggs for brains."

"You're wrong about him. He's just wound up like a clock spring. I recollect the story of how he was maybe eight or nine when his father got a Ute arrow in him up in the San Juan mountains. Colby held his pa in his arms for days before he died, then had to bury him. Took Colby two weeks to walk out on his own. They say he was never the same after that."

"A little crazy, is he?"

"Just stand back. Here he comes."

In his early thirties, Colby was a big muscular man with hard, weathered features and a jagged scar on his left cheek, his gunbelt loaded with cartridges, and two big irons in cut-down holsters slung low on his hips. There was sweat on his linen shirt under a black leather vest. He walked with catlike movement, as if every step was planned.

They watched through the window as Colby approached, and the lawman was getting nervous.

"He's got four brothers over in Socorro and just as tough, but Colby's the most dangerous."

They backed away a step as the big man entered.

Colby glanced at the empty cells and the strange look on the young deputy's face. He turned to the marshal as he pushed his Stetson back from his lined brow. His ice-blue eyes were shaded by dark brows, and he spoke in a deep, resonant voice that could chill any man.

"Caught him with a running iron. He put up a fight, and I had to kill him. His name's on papers in his vest pocket. I'll be back later to file a report."

The marshal was trying to swallow and couldn't, and he wiped his mouth with the back of his gnarled hand. Colby started for the door, and finally the marshal found his voice.

"Sit down a minute, Colby. I got to talk with you."

"I'm tired and hot, and I need a bath."

"While you was gone, the bank was robbed. A dozen of 'em with their faces covered. Three days ago."

"That so?"

"They got away in the rain with a heap of money. The clerk was wounded, but he lived through it. He knew Billy Keo right off on account of he'd met him in Texas when he was down that way visitin' his folks. Now the clerk admits he must have talked too much around Billy, bragging about his responsibility for all that money."

"Takes a man to admit a mistake."

"Well, he also recognized Miles and Mickey, both with scars, and Mickey having been nearly scalped once with half his hair gone. Bandannas couldn't hide them faces."

"I thought those two were in Yuma."

"Seems they busted out. Now there was also one fellow calling the shots, had gray eyes and a skinny nose. Could be they was all Keos."

"Didn't Kansas Grange run with them once?"

"The gunslinger? I think he's up in the Dakotas, but I ain't sure. But Colby, listen, I got to talk to you."

Colby lifted his hat to run his hand over his dirty hair, then pulled it down tight by tugging at the brim. Stretching wearily, Colby turned and moved into the open doorway, about to leave.

Sweat on his face, the marshal cleared his throat.

"You got to listen to me, Colby. The clerk, he got shot, and a customer, a young woman caught in there with him, was killed. She was your sister."

Stiff as stone, big shoulders hunched up, Colby couldn't move. His voice was raspy as his hands turned into fists. "*What?*"

"She didn't suffer none, Colby. It all happened too fast. We buried her out near the church. I couldn't wait no longer for you to get back, so I sent word to your brothers over at Socorro. They oughta be here any time now."

Slowly, Colby turned so they could see the hard set of his jaw and icy slits of his eyes. "Which one of them pulled the trigger?"

The marshal swallowed hard. "Well, the clerk says he was shot by the one who had to be Billy, but it was Mickey Keo what killed your sister. Now here are the handbills, got their descriptions and drawings of 'em. There's a reward out on Miles and Mickey."

The marshal handed him the reward posters, which Colby studied only a moment before sliding them inside his vest. Then the marshal stepped back to stand near his desk and slowly moved behind it as Colby's voice grew deeper.

"Why'd they open fire?"

"Seems they thought the clerk was reaching for a gun when he stepped behind the counter, but he says he was only tryin' to get some cover. However, he thinks they were planning to kill them anyway. Keos don't like to leave witnesses."

Colby's face darkened as he tugged at the brim of his Stetson. His eyes were so narrowed they were near hidden. Sweat beaded on his strong nose and dampened his day's growth of whiskers. His wide mouth was drawn into a tight, narrow line. He turned toward the open door with slow steps.

There was a long, terrible and breathless silence.

Then Colby Dancer slowly reached for the latch on the open door. He paused, his big shoulders hunched, and there was a long moment when an explosion seemed about to surface, yet Colby just released the latch and walked outside.

Colby stood on the boardwalk a long time, his hands in big fists at his sides. Then he slowly walked over to his sorrel gelding. He dropped the lead to the rustler's horse, wrapping it around the hitching rail.

He brought his mount around as he swung into the saddle like a cavalryman ready for war. Tall and straight, he didn't look back as he rode up the empty street toward the church on the far hill.

Along the street, faces appeared at doors and windows, and two men carefully came out of the store across the street, one keeping a foot just inside for safety.

Standing in his doorway, the marshal wiped his brow with relief as he turned to his deputy. "He's killin' himself from the inside out."

*   *   *   *   *

Colby and his four brothers had lost their father when Colby was small, and their mother had died a few years back, leaving no blood kin. They knew their mother's younger brother had run away as a boy and disappeared, leaving her elderly parents as her only relatives, and it was a painful letter they had to write about their only granddaughter.

After that fateful day in New Mexico Territory when they lost their sister, the brothers searched for the Keos from Texas north to the Canadian border for two years without success. It was Colby who settled in the Powder River country in Wyoming Territory. He took a job as range detective for the cattlemen, hunting rustlers, but in the back of his mind, he had a continuing thirst for vengeance.

One day in spring of 1879, he received a message from a friend of his, the sheriff down in Pocket, a small cow-town just north of Cheyenne. The letter said it was urgent. As Colby rode into the empty street of an evening, hunched over in the soft rain that dribbled from his hat band, he saw the express office with a missing door.

He reined up and leaned low in the saddle to have a look. In the back room where the vault was sitting, the walls had been sucked inward, as had the front door. There was heavy damage to the big walnut counter, but it had remained standing.

He reined about and rode over in the slush to the sheriff's office. Leaving his sorrel at the railing, he found the bearded lawman half asleep with his boots up on his desk.

When he saw Colby, he yawned and stretched, then sat up.

"You took your time gettin' here."

"What happened to the express office?"

"Well, sir, about a week ago, some fellahs come along in the middle of the night and tried to blow the vault, but one of 'em got killed on account of the dynamite went off afore he could get out of the back room. The vault never cracked, and the others got away with nothing, but we had a dead one on our hands. Billy Keo."

Colby was so startled, he sank down on a chair with his slicker crackling and rain dripping from his hat brim, his breath sucked right out of him.

"Yeah," the sheriff continued. "Billy Keo, one of the ones you was lookin' for all this time. I figure he had four others with him."

"How do you know it was Billy Keo?"

"He matched the handbill, and his sixgun had his initials on it. So did his saddle."

Colby drew a deep breath. For two years, he had lived for this moment, and now the man was dead. He sat numb as he listened to the sheriff.

"Seems Billy was using the name Billy Smith. He and four others had just delivered a stallion over at the Box Tree, not far from here. They'd come all the way from the Rockin' R at Dead Man's Creek, over in Montana Territory."

"Dead Man's Creek?"

"In a valley south of Butte City. Got a friend works at the prison up in Deer Lodge, and he's written me about it. Seems it's turned into an outlaw's hangout and right dangerous. Even the vigilantes don't go there. And the Rockin' R runs the valley."

"This Billy Keo, what did he look like?"

"Curly brown hair, pale eyes. Face pretty much like the handbill, but there wasn't much left of the rest of him. Could be the others headed back to the Rockin' R. Probably went up the Bozeman right past where you've been huntin' rustlers."

"And the Box Tree, did they have anything to say?"

"Just that Billy gave 'em the bill-of-sale, and nobody got a good look at the other four. They looked at the handbill and said it was him all right."

"Were any of 'em scarred?"

"Like I said, nobody had a look at the other four."

"You hear any more about Kansas Grange?"

"Just that he was over in Dakota, but I think you're barkin' up the wrong tree on him. I know what they was sayin' down in Slye, but I don't believe he ever run with the Keos. Now maybe he knew 'em, but that don't mean anything. Grange is a loner. What you're lookin' for is Keos."

"Well, whoever they were, maybe the rest of them headed back to the Rockin' R. I'd better mosey up there and have a look."

"Bad idea, Colby."

"I got to go."

"You'll be ridin' into a hornet's nest. Most of 'em will be wanted, maybe even some of the rustlers you couldn't catch, and there's no law there, so there's nobody you can count on. And I can tell you this, if you go ridin' in there, you ain't never comin' back."

"I got no choice, sheriff."

"Well, if you gotta go, maybe I can help. Billy had a bank draft in his pocket made out to a Melina Ramsey of the Rockin' R, wrote out for five hundred dollars for that stallion, payable at a bank in Butte City. Now if you want to deliver it, you might be able to get some information out of her."

"Thanks. I'll do that."

That night, Colby wrote to his youngest brother, Seth—the only one with a cool head—who was working in Denver. The next morning, a pack horse trailing, Colby headed up the Bozeman Trail. His sister's death was still a knot in his gut and he had never been able to face it, but he thought of her a lot, always seeing her as still alive.

She had been small with blue eyes and a button nose, smiling up at him. "You're the wild one, Colby. The rest of us always had more sense."

Tears stung his eyes, but he still refused to break down, not until the dozen men involved were dead or behind bars. And he was going to give personal attention to Mickey Keo.

Colby headed north, days passing into weeks, and when he was but a week away from his destination, he slowed his pace, not wanting to rush in like a crazy man.

Meanwhile, business was flourishing in Dead Man's Creek, set in a vast, lush valley surrounded by high, forested mountains with a canyon entrance at the east end where the creek passed through.

The town spread on both sides of the wooden bridge. On the south side, a saloon, a gambling hall, and a questionable two-story hotel were lively with restless, dangerous men.

On the north side, stores and the livery supplied the valley ranchers. Buildings on either side of the creek were faded from winter, and the boardwalks were cracked and warped.

At the west end of the green valley, the falls crashed down through a gorge and into rapids, then hurried south toward town. Some distance east of the falls, the Ramsey ranch house was nestled in a stand of aspens on the highest of the rolling hills, not far from the sparkling water where cottonwoods, rocks and brush lined its banks.

Two of the hands were sitting on the corral fence down by

the sheds and bunkhouse in the early sunlight. One was long past eighty, missing a lot of teeth, his white handlebar mustache down to his jutting chin, clear blue eyes scanning the mountains as he spat tobacco juice.

"I figure that cat will be back, all right. It's laid out its territory."

The younger hand, mid-twenties, his round face dotted with freckles, pushed his hat back. "But I can't figure how she missed that shot. I ain't never seen her miss anything before."

"Mitts, don't you worry about Mrs. Ramsey. She can out-shoot any one of us with a rifle."

"You think the boss is ever comin' back, Hobbs?"

"Maybe. Maybe not. But until he does, you'd better stay out of her way."

"She's always tryin' to prove she's as good as any man. Why is that, Hobbs? Why can't she settle down and be a woman? I mean, she's real pretty when she don't know you're lookin'. And she wears all them heavy clothes to hide herself."

"Ain't safe for her to show any sign of weakness. Not with them outlaws hangin' around the valley."

"Or workin' for her. Why you figure she has to have them Jones boys around? They give me the jitters."

"Mr. Ramsey hired them and Billy afore he took off. And I reckon she figures she needs men like that to keep the rest away from here."

As the two men talked, Melina Ramsey stared out the second story window of her house, and the town, thirty miles east, was getting lively as Saturday wore on past noon.

In a shack behind the saloon, Max Jones and his cousin Skip were just waking up.

Max was in his mid-forties, husky, bearded, his pale brown eyes ever glowering, and he was usually sweaty and dirty. Skip was two years younger, thinner, clean-shaven with mean features, and a lot neater. Both men had curly brown hair.

Max rolled over on his bunk, wiping the damp from his furrowed brow. "I just had one lousy dream. About Billy."

"You got to stop that. Weren't your fault."

"That dynamite stick was sweatin'. I never should have let him try to use it."

"It was the only one we had left, and he's the one knew how to handle it, remember? We didn't have no choice, Max. Just be glad we had the sense to get down behind that counter when he lit the fuse."

"I reckon you're right, Skip."

"All we got to do right now is make up a story for Melina Ramsey."

"I'd like to do more than that."

Skip chuckled. "She'd blow your head off if you looked sideways at her. Heck, maybe she'd like me better. I ain't been to school like you, but I got a lot more muscle."

"All in your head."

"Don't be puttin' me down, Max. I get real mad. Besides, we got nothin' to worry about. She pays us plenty good."

"She's sittin' on all that grass with all them cattle."

"And a man who's gonna come home someday. And if he don't, Purvis is going to take over. You know how Purvis thinks he's so much better than us anyhow. His nose is always stuck up in the air like he's smelling the ceiling."

"Well, I ain't scared of Ramsey or Purvis. And I might just go a-courtin' one of these days. Got to be a woman under all them clothes she wears to keep us from havin' a look."

"Max, your head's on crooked. Besides, we're gonna have enough trouble explainin' to her why Billy ain't here with the bankdraft."

"I'm gonna tell her we was set on by outlaws, and Billy died with it in his pocket but we couldn't go back. If it shows up, that's our story. We're here, and the sheriff ain't."

"Sure, Max, but I'm right sorry we hooked up with Lacey and his ugly partner. I never got no sleep on the trail, wonderin' if they was gonna slit our throats. They're animals."

"Yeah, well, when they run out of gamblin' money, they'll leave, all right."

"I sure hope so." Skip stretched lazily and scratched at his soiled undershirt. Then he scratched his dirty hair. "We both need a bath. Purvis's got some new sportin' ladies over at the Silver Dollar, and he promised to get a room for us at his hotel. And I figure this time we'll beat that roulette wheel of his. Now come on, this is our holiday, remember? And we're safe here."

"You're right about that. Ain't nobody's got the guts to follow us into Dead Man's Creek."

CHAPTER TWO

O n Monday morning, Melina Ramsey made certain that Hobbs and Mitts were with her on the front porch when she saw the two Jones cousins returning.

She stood waiting, shaded from the sun, her long black hair tied back with a ribbon from her pretty, oval face. Wearing a coat over her muslin blouse and heavy skirt, she folded her arms and leaned on a post, watching as the men dismounted at the corrals.

Mitts grimaced. "They sure is mean lookin'."

"I'm not afraid," she said.

Hobbs had his coat back from his holster, but they knew there was no way he could take the Jones boys or any of the other gunmen who haunted the valley. He spat tobacco juice and worked his mouth as he studied the two men.

Melina's large, dark brown eyes were hard set under long lashes, but her breath was short. It was important that she stay calm, in charge, and she straightened as the two gunmen walked toward the ranch house. Little needles seemed to be digging into her spine.

Max and Skip tipped their hats and came to stand below in the dirt, looking up at where she stood on the porch. She was stern with her feet apart. They had been gone a long time, and she was not happy to see them.

"Where's Billy?" she asked.

"Well, it's a long story," Max said, a smoke dangling from his lip. "It'd come out better over a cup of coffee."

"The cook will take care of you at the cook shack."

"All right then, Mrs. Ramsey. We delivered that stallion down to the Powder River country. Billy, he gave 'em the bill of sale and got the draft, and we started on our way back."

"And?"

"We was jumped on the Bozeman by a bunch of outlaws. Billy was shot out of the saddle, and we just barely got away with our hides."

"And the bank draft?"

Taken aback by her coolness over Billy's death, Max studied her a long moment before answering. He tried to keep his eyes from wandering up and down her shape, which wasn't hard since she was covered up as usual.

"Reckon it died with Billy, unless somebody found his body out there and took it off 'im. But if you write that fella down at the Box Tree, I figure he'd send another one."

"I'll do that."

"He sure was happy with that stallion."

"Thank you, Max. Now go on and get some rest."

The gunmen nodded and walked back towards the corrals, waiting until they were out of earshot. Then Max puffed on his smoke and spoke in a low voice.

"That's one handsome woman. I'd sure like to get a hold of

her, all right. I figure a roll in the hay with Melina Ramsey has got to be mighty fine."

"Ain't smart, Max. Ramsey comes back, he'll have your hide. And Purvis would skin you alive. Besides, this is the best hideout we ever had. We pretty much do as we damn well please around here. You want to ruin everything?"

"I'd like to take it over right now, and to heck with Ramsey or Purvis."

"You're forgettin' somethin'. There's six other men on this ranch who ain't gonna sit back and watch."

"They're nothin' but cowhands. Mitts ain't got no sense, and Hobbs is too old. None of 'em are fancy with a gun."

"Yeah, well, Purvis figures Mrs. Ramsey's a real lady and she don't make no trouble for him in town. He figures her stayin' out of it keeps the rest of the ranchers off his back and the law out of the valley, so you go causin' her any mischief, he's liable to just blow our heads off. Not to mention what Ramsey would do when he got back."

Max grinned. "It might be worth it."

While the two men settled into the empty bunkhouse, Colby was at Indian Station, a stage relay and post office, a five-days' ride from the valley. Weary, he had put up for the night in the tack room, and in the morning, he was at the old couple's table. The wife was busy at the stove, making more coffee.

"I see by the sign over there that you have the mail contract," Colby said to the husband.

"Wasn't renewed. Mail's been shifted over to Pine Ridge route. Dead Man's Creek just got the last mail from Indian Station. Sent out yesterday. From now on, they got to go eighty miles from here to Pine Ridge."

"Stage still be coming this way?"

"Not much longer. We're closing our station as soon as we get the word. Seems they want to break trail near Pine Ridge and over at Willow Creek, where they just found gold. And somethin' to do with the Utah & Northern comin' up from Utah. The legislature done voted against the subsidy in January, but I hear tell they're gonna have a special session in July, and it could go through this time."

"Sounds like politics."

"Sure is. You wonder what goes on in a place with a pretty name like Helena that can't get no business done."

"So the railroad won't be swinging this far over?"

"Don't seem like it. But I got my own opinion as to why, and it's all got to do with Dead Man's Creek."

Colby downed his coffee. "Because of its reputation?"

"That's right. Nothin' but outlaws there, and any railroad man worth his salt is gonna bypass this area."

Colby thanked them for the meal and spent an hour cutting wood for the old couple, using a chipped ax and a saw with half its teeth gone.

Later that morning, the wind blowing strong, he was outside saddling up when he saw another rider coming from the north.

The man was lean and looked to be in his early sixties, wearing a white collar, his gray hair close-cropped under a small brimmed hat, and a gunbelt half hidden under his dark coat. He had dark gleaming, dangerous eyes and a wide mouth in a thin face. Colby would have taken him for a gunman and not a man of the cloth.

The man reined his bay to a halt and leaned wearily on the

saddle. "Are you one of those lost souls from Dead Man's Creek?"

"That where you're headed?"

"Soon's my horse gets a good rest. He's footsore. But you didn't answer my question."

"Are you a preacher?"

"That's what they call me. And I've come to do God's work in that devil's pit. Now, do you have a name?"

"You get to Dead Man's Creek, you'd best be careful who you ask that question."

The preacher straightened in the saddle with a frown. "You sure are a friendly cuss."

Colby swung astride. "I'd take it kindly if you'd say a prayer for me, because it ain't likely I'm comin' out alive."

Turning his sorrel toward the western mountains, Colby lifted his hat to smooth his long hair, then pulled it down tight on his brow.

The preacher removed his own hat, gray hair blowing in the wind, calling after him. "God bless you, son."

Turning to the elderly couple, the preacher bowed and greeted them. "My horse and I are weary. I hope you have a place for us tonight."

"Sure enough, preacher," the old man said.

Exhausted and chilled by the wind, the preacher swung down and led his horse over to the corrals. After unsaddling and rubbing his horse down, he joined the couple for a noon meal. They were curious about his sixgun and collar, but they were too polite to question him.

"Perhaps," the preacher said, "you can tell me the name of that young man who rode out this morning."

"Colby Dancer."

The preacher's blazing eyes narrowed to slits, his mouth twisting. "Glory be."

*   *   *   *   *

The following Friday morning, Colby reined up on the ridge overlooking the valley. He could see distant herds of cattle and horses, and he studied the town where it straddled the creek.

He could be riding to his death, but he had made himself a promise at his sister's grave, and he wasn't turning back until he found the twelve ruthless men who had caused her death.

At least four of them could be right down below.

When he reached the valley in the late afternoon, he rode along the north side of the wide creek which was certainly more than a creek. He saw the saloon, gambling hall and sleazy hotel to his left across the bridge, but he turned up the street on his right, into the "respectable" part of town, but even there, he saw a gunsmith shop which doubled as a land office.

Four rough-looking men paused on the boardwalk outside the general store to watch him all the way to the livery. Outside the barn in a lean-to, a black smithy, shirt off and big muscles gleaming with sweat, was banging away on a horseshoe as twilight fell.

"Need your horse shod, mister?"

Colby dismounted, wondering how many men this husky man had downed for making fun of his being a black blacksmith.

"No, he's fit. You run the livery?"

"Yeah, my name's Jackson. Two bits a night for hay and grain, and you get a stall. You want to sleep in the loft, I throw that in, but you have to watch yourself. A lot of thieves around here."

"All right," Colby said, tossing the coin which Jackson caught easily. "I could use some information."

"About the town, that's free. About people, it'll cost you. Man has to make a livin'."

"Tell me about the town."

"You cross over that bridge, you'll run into perdition. Some real bad ones over there. They come with pocketfuls of money. When they run out, they leave until they get some more. Folks this side of the creek had a town going about a year before them places sprung up on the south side. Purvis and his bunch took over and made a home for outlaws, and that's a fact. A lot of folks left on account of they was scared. Only about sixty of 'em still here. Even the sawmill over by the north mountains, it closed down."

"And Purvis?"

"That's two bits."

Colby shook his head and surrendered the coin.

Jackson grunted. "Colby owns most everything south of the creek includin' the Silver Dollar and the hotel, and he's got some soiled doves. He has some thirty hardcases at a time over there. But ole Purvis, he likes to think he's respectable. Speaks kind of pretty, too."

"And what about Melina Ramsey?"

Jackson used a pair of long tongs to hold the horseshoe in the hot coals, sweat running down his round face. "Well, that'll be another two bits."

"I can find out somewhere else for free."

"Yeah, but you won't know how much of it is true."

Colby shook his head again, grinned as he tossed the coin, then pushed his hat back. "So there really are thieves around

19

here. All right, give—and make it worth two bits or I'll push your face in."

The smithy brought the horseshoe back to the anvil with a chuckle. "All by your lonesome?"

Colby sat on the bench in the shade of the lean-to, his sorrel nuzzling his shoulder, and he waited impatiently. Finally Jackson paused in his hammering.

"Well, she's in her late twenties, I think. Lou Ramsey took over the valley in late '77. Brought up a big herd he'd picked up in Colorado and Wyomin' Territory. Then last fall, he brung his wife and son up here."

"Son?"

"About nine years old. Don't think he's hers, though. Anyhow, a few weeks later, he was gone, and she's been runnin' things ever since. Some even think she did away with him just to have the ranch to herself and the boy."

"That what you think?"

"Well, it's what some people figured on account of she's so tough. But she was getting a letter about every few weeks from him, by way of Indian Station. Funny thing is, the storekeeper says she ain't had one in over two months. Unless it's in the batch that came in yesterday."

Colby turned to throw the left stirrup over the saddle, and he set about uncinching his sorrel. The animal heaved with relief. The chill of evening was coming fast, and it pawed the dirt.

Jackson rested his hammer. "Ole Purvis, he figures he's going to be the next he-bull out at the Rockin' R. Anybody else tries to take a shine to Mrs. Ramsey, he cuts 'em off short. Most of 'em give Purvis a wide berth. Oh, he talks mighty fine, but he's got crazy eyes."

"Sounds like I oughta have a look at this Purvis."

"You got a name?"

"Colby Dancer."

"That so? They say you're goin' to the devil in a hand basket. Word is you hunt rustlers down at the Powder River and bring most of 'em in across the saddle. Now, you can figure a few of the ones you missed are probably south of the bridge right now. When they find out you're here, I wouldn't give a plug nickel for your bein' around much longer."

"I ain't got time to worry about them. Now, this Melina Ramsey, does she come to town much?"

"Not very often. And I'll tell you somethin', nobody ever gives her any sass, and she don't make no trouble for them south of the creek. It's almost like they made a deal to stay out of each other's way."

"What about Billy Keo?"

"Heard of him. But if he's here, he ain't usin' that name."

"And Kansas Grange?"

"You got to be funnin' me. They say he's so mean, fire shoots out of his ears, and I ain't seen nobody like that around here. Besides, I heard he was dead."

"Then how about some gunmen that work for Mrs. Ramsey and just got back from delivering a stallion down near Cheyenne?"

"That's another two bits."

Colby shook his head, annoyed, but he fished around for the coin until he found it, then tossed it over. The smithy caught it in his big fist and tossed it into a tin cup with the rest. Then he put the horseshoe in cold water as he continued.

"They work for her, all right. Max and Skip Jones, and Billy

Smith, all cousins, I think. Lou Ramsey hired them last fall, just afore he took off. Maybe he wanted some tough ones to watch out for her."

"They in town?"

"Max and Skip got back about a week ago with a couple mean looking fellahs, but I didn't see Billy. Now Max, he's got a beard and's pretty husky. Skip, he's skinnier and shaves clean. All three are plenty fast, and that's a fact. Tomorrow's Saturday, so they'll be comin' in to town."

"Anything else?"

"If there was, it'd cost you, but no, that's about it. You'll find out the rest if you tangle with 'im. I'll make a real nice coffin for you. And I'll get the barber to lay you out for half price."

"You're real friendly. Well, I'll put up for the night. How do I get out to the Rockin' R? And it'd better not cost me."

Jackson grinned and wiped his brow with the back of his big hand. "Well, you cross the creek and head west on the wagon road. Stay on the south side of the creek because on the north side, you get nothin' but rocks and brush. But you'll see her gate about ten miles west of town. Now, mind you, there ain't no fence, just a big sign on two posts, but it marks the boundary straight to Black Butte on your left and the mountains on the right, across the creek. Anybody lets their cattle across that line, they're in a lot of trouble."

"So there are other ranchers."

"And a couple farmers, but she's the boss around here. And as far as the road out there goes, ain't much cover on it. You don't want to be seen, you stay close to the creek where the cottonwoods are lined up, or cross to the rocky side."

At Jackson's suggestion, Colby ate supper at the Red Feather, the only saloon on the north side of the creek, with Jackson joining him. As they walked out onto the creaking boardwalk in the moonlight, they could hear noise from south of the bridge where lamps burned in front of the buildings.

Colby listened intently. "You said two other men came back with the Jones boys."

"Two of the meanest lookin' fellahs you ever saw. One of 'em was called Lacey. Tall, all muscle, black mustache. Other had a thick beard. They'd slit your throat for a glass of whiskey. That's all I know. And that one's free."

"Lacey. I know about Lacey. I've chased him a time or two. His friend is probably the fellow that was ridin' with 'im when they got away. Rustlers for sure, but I could never catch them."

"They'll figure you're here for one reason, and that's to drag 'em back to a hanging. And you're outnumbered. You're crazy, Dancer."

Colby turned and walked along the creaking boardwalk toward the bridge, the moon casting his shadow before him. There were a few horses in front of the hotel on the right where lamps were burning in some of the rooms.

Between the hotel and the creek was the single level gambling hall with several men at the tables.

On the left was a large saloon with a second story, and behind it were tents and shacks. Further along were a series of corrals and sheds with many horses inside.

Colby's boots clumped all too loudly on the bridge.

CHAPTER THREE

Colby's heart was thumping, but he continued his walk toward the lamps burning in front of the swinging doors of the Silver Dollar. Smoke curled out into the night, and he could hear voices inside.

He paused by the bat-wing doors and peered into the hazy room. The only customers were two bearded men at a side table, arguing and playing cards, while a red headed woman in a red dress was draped over a chair between them. The bartender was a fat, greasy man with several chins, and he was cleaning glasses.

Another man was behind the bar, counting money. In his mid forties, he had a thin nose and pale blond hair, and he wasn't wearing a coat, his white shirt spotless under a fancy red vest. He had a haughty look about him, as if he belonged some place fancier. He was obviously the boss. Purvis.

All eyes were fixed on Colby as he entered.

The woman stood up, adjusting the red feathers in her auburn hair, and she came around the table. She had a weary smile, the powder spotty on her cheeks, bruises on her left arm, and she walked as if her feet were hurting in her satin shoes.

"Welcome to the Silver Dollar."

Colby walked over to the bar with her at his heels, and they both leaned on the polished walnut. Behind the bar, there was a huge mirror with gilded edge hanging behind rows of glasses and bottles.

Colby had to start somewhere, and he might as well start a fire with a dead man. He stood with his hands at his sides, watching the men and woman as he spoke.

"I'm looking for Billy Keo."

The bartender stopped polishing the glass. The man with the money folded it and gazed at him with blazing gray eyes as he spoke in a sneering voice, his obvious attitude that he was too good to be standing around here with the likes of Colby.

"My name is Purvis, and I own this place and the hotel. And the gambling hall. One of the rules around here is no one makes trouble, or they have to leave. We've had no killings since we opened. And there's nobody in town named Keo."

The woman took Colby's arm. "Why don't you come with me?"

"Sorry."

She gave him a weary smile, didn't seem disappointed, and went back to the men at the table. Colby leaned on the bar and looked directly at Purvis, but the man didn't flinch. Colby was disappointed, because only a few men would know that Billy Keo was dead, and he had hoped Purvis was one of them.

Looking as ornery as he knew possible, Colby then spoke in his deep, resonant voice. "You see Billy Keo, you tell him Colby Dancer's looking for him."

Purvis's face went dark and his eyes squinched.

Colby turned and walked out of the saloon, heart pounding so loud he could hear it. He had spread the word. Now all heck was going to break loose.

The chill of the night grew more intense.

As he crossed back to the north side, he saw everything was sealed up and dark. These people knew how to avoid trouble, and he didn't blame them. Some sixty townspeople would be no match for the outlaws south of the bridge.

At the barn, Jackson was waiting with a big grin. "I didn't think I'd see you again."

"You can give thanks when you go to church."

"We got no church here."

"I have a feeling you're going to have one mighty soon."

Jackson grunted. "That so?"

"Preacher's coming."

"That ain't all."

They turned to see two men walking toward them in the moonlight and keeping to the dry mud of the wide street. One was tall with a mustache, the other had a thick black beard. They looked dangerous.

"Lacey and his friend," Jackson said. "Well, you asked for it, and that's a fact. Me, I'm turnin' in. Got me a room back of the barn. They take you down, I'll throw in the coffin for free."

"You're all heart."

Jackson disappeared into the barn where a lamp burned just inside the door. Colby had never felt so lonely, but he stood on the boardwalk, his coat back from his twin holsters, hands at his side, watching the two men approach.

Lacey was the leader, that was obvious, and Jackson was right. This was an ugly man with an ugly soul, looked like he'd slit your throat without hesitation, and likely enjoy it.

Right hand near his holster, Lacey took a stand in the street with his feet apart. The other man moved over to Colby's left.

"Now then," Lacey said with a sneer. "Purvis tells me you're Colby Dancer, that yellow-bellied man hunter from the Powder River. Why, you're lower than a snake's belly. You tracked down some of my friends, killed 'em dead. I don't take kindly to that."

"I don't think you got any friends."

Lacey drew himself up. "Mister, we got us a rule south of the creek. No killin'. But that don't apply on the north side, no, sir, and I figure I'm goin' to gut-shoot you about now."

Colby spoke quietly. "I tracked the two of you on the Powder River, but that ain't why I'm here. All I want is Billy Keo."

"He's dead," Lacey said.

"And how would you know that if you wasn't in Pocket breaking into that vault when Billy was killed?"

"You got a big mouth, Dancer."

"Since you're about to blow me away, you might as well give me the truth."

Lacey snickered. "Yeah, we were in Pocket. Billy was supposed to know all about dynamite, but he didn't know enough to get out of the way in time."

"Jones boys in on it?"

"I'm finished talking, Dancer."

From the corner of his eye, Colby could see that the bearded man over to his left was getting restless. Getting them both was near impossible, and he didn't want to die before his job was finished.

"Go ahead," Lacey said. "I'll give you the edge."

"I got no time for you."

"I ain't givin' you no choice, Dancer."

"Then make your play."

Lacey smiled, his eyes gleaming. The chill of night was crisp. There was no wind. Silence surrounded them. The sky was dotted with shining stars and graced with the moon. The icy cold was biting at their faces and hands.

Colby could feel his heart expanding with pressure. It wasn't likely he could take them both. They looked plenty fast, and they knew what they were doing.

Drawing a deep breath, his fingers flexing, Colby waited, watching Lacey's eyes. And it was now!

Lacey's hand moved swift and sure, but as he drew and fired, Colby was already firing back. Their bullets crossed, and Lacey was hit in the chest. The man staggered back as Colby spun to fire at the other man, even as the man shot at him.

The outlaw was hit in the shoulder, and he kept firing as Colby danced aside and dropped to the boardwalk, firing again. The man gasped, a bullet in his throat, and he staggered backwards, arms flailing.

As the dead man hit the dirt, a rifle boomed right over Colby's head, hurting his ears, just as Lacey's bullet went wild past Colby's chin.

Colby fell back against the wall, six-guns hot in his hands as he saw Lacey spun around by the rifle slug, and then the outlaw dropped to the ground and rolled, blood spurting from his chest between his fingers.

Lacey kicked twice and then was as dead as his partner.

Standing just inside the doorway, Jackson peered outside "You all right, Dancer?"

"You sure took your time."

"You was doin' all right. But anybody asks, you got 'em both. I have to live in this town, and I can't be takin' sides."

"That sounded like a buffalo gun."

"Sharps. Yeah, I done a bit of huntin' for the railroad down in Wyomin'. Made enough to build this barn. And I aim to keep it, so you just get them two out of here."

"I'm goin' to bed."

"Well, I reckon the barber will get 'em. I see a light just went on in his shack across the street. He needs the money, and the town pays him."

Colby got to his feet, his middle churning. He would never have admitted it, but taking any life was brutal to his insides and his conscience.

Jackson came forward. "Hurry up. I'm closin' this door right now."

After a night's rest in the empty loft, Colby saddled up before dawn. The dead men were gone. It was Saturday morning, and he wasn't looking to run into anyone else right now.

Instead of crossing over to ride west along the creek on the wagon road, he could see the water was easily forded, so he stayed on the north side with the trees for cover. The going was tougher with the rocky ground and thick clumps of brush, but he wanted to surprise the men at the Rockin' R.

Riding west in the early sunlight, he tried to focus only on the job at hand. The rolling, green valley was still caressed with dew in all directions, and the air was fresh, clean as a whistle. The surrounding mountains were dark with forest and rising high against the haze of the horizons.

He could see the canyon where the creek came into the valley through a gorge from the east, and he felt trapped here, knowing he could die before the next sunup.

He saw trails leading to other ranches with distant cattle, but he wasn't prepared for the vast herds on the Rockin' R. By the time he saw the arch on the other side of the creek, he could see hundreds of head in the distance in all directions, and soon he realized there were thousands of head of cattle, mostly cows with calves.

Elk tracks led from the creek toward the northern mountains. Buzzards circled in the distance.

There were two riders on the other side of the creek, following the wagon road. He reined up in the trees until they passed.

He wasn't aware it was the two Jones boys heading back to town for their Saturday night. Skip was singing, "Oh, Susanna," and Max was complaining about his voice.

When they reached town late that afternoon, Skip could hardly wait to get back to the Silver Dollar and the women. Max was more casual about it, and they both walked into the Silver Dollar where a dozen men were playing cards at the tables. Three painted women were busy among them.

At the bar, Max leaned on the hard walnut and ordered whiskey from the barkeep while Skip called to Purvis.

"Hey, where's the redhead?"

"She's busy," Purvis said, coming over to them and facing them with a book in hand. "The two of you ever work out there?"

Skip grinned, sipping his drink. "They ain't got the guts to make us do much of anything."

"Where's Lacey and his partner?" Max asked, looking around. "They owe me some money."

Purvis made a face. "You won't get it now. They both crossed the bridge last night and took on Colby Dancer."

Max stiffened. "Dancer? The rustler bulldog?"

"Yes, and Lacey and his partner are both dead. Dancer's on his way out to the Rockin' R. One of the boys saw him leave town this morning."

Skip and Max turned to each other in dismay, and finally Skip wiped his mouth. "I didn't think anybody could take Lacey."

Max lowered his voice. "That means he's after us."

"He was asking for Billy," Purvis said.

"He don't know nothin'," Skip said. "We'll tell him Billy lied to us, telling us he was a cousin, and we believed him, that's all."

Purvis flipped the pages of his account book. "Maybe he knows Billy is dead."

"Not a chance," Max said. "Billy was blown to bits."

Skip frowned. "At least we think he was. We lit out so fast, we didn't see much of anything."

"Just the same," Max said, "ain't likely anyone knows yet."

"Before you go back to the ranch," Purvis said, "I assume you will be picking up their mail at the store."

"If there's any."

"I want you to bring it by here first."

Max downed his whiskey. "Maybe we'll hear from Miles and Mickey. What's takin' 'em so long, anyhow? They should have been here by now."

Skip laughed. "You know Mickey, he loves the women."

"Yeah, but he scares the heck out of me," Max said. "I can't stand to look at him. If we hadn't come along, that Apache would have finished the job. But he sure looks ugly with his hat off. I don't see how women can stand it."

Purvis poured them more whiskey as Max rolled a smoke, but he didn't like them. He felt all of his relatives were beneath him. They had no education, no smarts, no sensitivity. But he sure did agree with them on one thing—Mickey Keo could scare the heck out of anyone.

* * * * *

While Mickey and Miles Keo caused havoc in Pine Ridge, Purvis and the Jones boys were still at the Silver Dollar in Dead Man's Creek, and Colby was still riding west.

It was late afternoon when Colby saw the ranch buildings and corrals.

The two-story ranch house was set in a stand of aspen, little round leaves quaking in the wind, on a rise some distance from the corrals and outbuildings. Standing by the bunkhouse were two men, one old and one young, their horses saddled and nudging them. As he reined up by them, the old timer looked him over and spat tobacco juice.

"My name's Hobbs. I'm foreman here. And this is Mitts."

"Name's Dancer. From Wyoming Territory."

"Colby Dancer?"

Uneasy that his name was recognized, Colby nodded as he leaned on the horn and glanced toward the house. Hobbs looked to him like a man who rode for the brand and would not put up with any trouble, but Colby was on a mission.

"Jones boys here?"

"No, it's Saturday. They always go to town."

"I'd like to see Mrs. Ramsey."

"We ain't hirin' till fall roundup."

"I'm carrying a bankdraft for her, for a stallion delivered a couple weeks ago down on the Bar Tree, near Cheyenne."

"I'll give it to her."

"The sheriff asked me to deliver it in person."

Hobbs' white mustache twitched and he tugged at it, glancing toward the house. "Mitts, you go tell Mrs. Ramsey. We'll be along shortly."

The young cowboy mounted and rode up to the house, glancing back over his shoulder. Hobbs mounted and sat quiet in the saddle, which seemed molded to him.

"Mr. Dancer, I don't know how you got that bankdraft, but you got to know there are two Jones cousins on this ranch what said they was waylaid by outlaws that killed Billy Smith, and Billy was carrying that draft. Now you show up with a different story, I figure your life ain't worth two bits."

Colby had to grin, if only for a second. "Well, the smithy said it wasn't worth a plug nickel. I guess my chances are getting better."

"Yeah, you young fellahs can joke around, but when you get to my age, you'll have a little more sense."

"Such as?"

"Leavin' that draft with me and headin' back to Wyomin' as fast as that sorrel can take you."

"I come a long way, and I'm in no hurry."

"Some folks might think if the Jones boys is tellin' the truth, you was with the outlaws that got Billy."

"What do you think?"

Hobbs spat. "I wouldn't believe the Jones boys if they was sittin' on a stack of Bibles in the middle of a church and ringing the bell while they was swimmin' in Holy Water with a bunch of nuns holdin' their hands and the priest givin' 'em the blessing."

Hobbs turned his horse, and they rode up toward the ranch house where Mitts was standing on the covered porch, talking through a partially opened door.

Then the youth came to the steps. "Hobbs, Mrs. Ramsey wants you and Mr. Dancer to come inside."

Colby didn't know what to expect, but he swung down along with the foreman, and they tied the reins to the hitching rail. As Mitts left, the two men walked up the creaking steps to the porch. The door was still partially open, and Hobbs led the way inside.

The front room had a saddle on a wood frame, leather furniture, ropes, bridles and hides on the walls, and no fire in the big stone hearth. From the other room to their left came the scent of strong coffee. Over to the right, they could see a stairway leading from a darker room with a back door.

Both men stood with hats in hand near the empty fireplace, and Colby felt a sudden chill as he sensed someone was entering the room from behind him.

Wearing a shawl over a blouse and a dark skirt with a sixgun strapped at her hip, a woman walked past him carrying a tray bearing cups of hot coffee. She ignored them as she moved to set the tray on a small, round table in the center of the circle of chairs.

There was no sign of the boy.

Colby couldn't see much of her face as her long dark hair was hiding all but a pert nose from his view. She was tall and obviously slim under her heavy clothes, and she moved with grace, almost as if she was on a dance floor.

Then she straightened and turned toward him, and Colby

saw her astonishing, wonderful face. He could only stare.

Her dark brown eyes were gleaming under long, thick lashes, her skin smooth with the color of peaches on high cheek bones. Her full lips were set in a firm line as if she never smiled. Despite her practiced arrogance, she was unbearably beautiful.

"I'm Melina Ramsey. And you're Colby Dancer?"

"Yes, ma'am. The sheriff of Pocket, down in Wyoming Territory just north of Cheyenne, he sent this up to you."

He reached inside his vest to retrieve the draft, and he handed it over as she came closer. He caught the scent of roses, and he swallowed, watching her slim white fingers cross his rough hand as she retrieved the paper.

She held it in both hands, gazing at it. "I didn't expect to see this. Please, have some coffee."

They sat down facing the table and each other, and Hobbs was first to reach for a cup. "I got to tell you about this fellow, Mrs. Ramsey."

"Mr. Dancer's reputation is well-known. What I want to know is, where did the sheriff get this draft?"

"Five men tried to rob the express office one night in Pocket several weeks ago. Billy Keo was killed fooling around with some dynamite, and the others took off without any money. The sheriff found the draft in his vest, only the papers say it was delivered to a Billy Smith."

Melina listened to his words in dark silence, and she looked at Hobbs, who was shaking his head.

"You're sayin'," Hobbs said, "that Billy Smith was really the outlaw, Billy Keo?"

"He was identified from a handbill."

Melina seemed to shiver as she stared into her coffee.

Colby lifted a cup from the tray and leaned back. "Sheriff figures whoever came down to Wyoming with Billy was in on it. And that means Max and Skip Jones. And since they were all three supposed to be cousins, it looks mighty suspicious. I figure all three are Keos."

Melina reached for her cup and held it in both hands, then spoke with a chill in her voice. "Do you have proof?"

"No, ma'am."

"Then I'm asking you to finish your coffee and leave."

"I'd like to talk to the Jones boys first."

Hobbs sipped his coffee and turned. "Mr. Dancer, are you plannin' to kill those boys?"

"Maybe."

Melina stood up, and the men scrambled to their feet.

"I won't have any gunfights on my ranch."

"Uh, Mrs. Ramsey," Hobbs said, "remember what we was talking about?"

CHAPTER FOUR

M elina Ramsey glanced at her foreman. "Yes, and the answer is still no. You see, Mr. Dancer, Mr. Hobbs thinks I need a bodyguard, but that's a sign of weakness, and I am not interested. So, good day, gentlemen."

Hobbs twirled his hat in his hand, set down his cup and headed for the door. Colby stood a moment longer, studying her face and fiery eyes.

"You know, ma'am, Hobbs is right. You ain't safe with the Jones boys on the ranch."

Her chin went up, her hand resting on her holster. "I can take care of myself, Mr. Dancer."

Colby shrugged, set his cup on the table, and pulled on his Stetson, tugging at the wide brim. He looked her over so long and hard, she drew herself up in anger.

"Good day, Mr. Dancer. If you're not afraid, Mr. Hobbs will find a bunk for you, that is, if you don't mind spending Saturday night out here."

Colby smiled, then turned with Hobbs just as there was a

pounding on the door. The foreman opened the door and Mitts came hurrying inside, face pink and eyes round.

"Red just rode in. His old hound tangled with that cougar and got killed. Red's mighty upset, but he shot the cat on the run, and it left a trail of blood. Headed up Red Rock Canyon. Now we got to go after it."

"Too late tonight," Hobbs said. "We'll ride out first thing in the morning. Sure wish we had some other dogs around so they could tree it."

Melina came forward. "I'll be going with you. And Mr. Dancer, if you have nothing else to do, you can ride along. We can't have that wounded cat running around loose. No telling what it will do."

Colby nodded, understanding the gravity, and he was about to leave when he heard footsteps running down the stairs in the next room. A young boy in his nightshirt, yellow hair a mess, left arm in a sling, blue eyes round and wide in his freckled face, appeared before them.

"Hey Mom, can I go with you?"

Melina's harsh stance softened. "Your arm needs another week in that sling. You were lucky it wasn't broken."

"But if Mr. Dancer's there, it'll be all right."

She stiffened, watching the boy's smile turned on Colby Dancer, and she didn't like it. It was obvious the boy had been listening from the stairs.

"There'll be no more discussion on this, Tommy."

"I never get to do nothin'."

"*Anything.*"

Colby couldn't help but notice the difference between the boy and Melina Ramsey. He didn't figure she was the boy's mother, not with her near-black hair and dark eyes.

The boy's rosy cheeks and round face were a delight, even though he was furious with his mother. Finally, he started to turn away, but then he paused, looking at Colby.

"We hear about you all the time, Mr. Dancer. You're a real gunfighter."

Colby was uneasy at the admiration. He had never been around children in his adult life, and he squirmed under the boy's steady smile. He found himself grinning at him anyway.

"Tommy," Melina said, "go upstairs now."

"Mr. Dancer, will you teach me to draw fast?"

"Tommy, that's enough."

"Gee whiz." Making a face, the boy turned and disappeared into the next room, and then they heard his reluctant footsteps on the stairs.

Hobbs grinned. "That boy's going to be a real hand someday, but he's been bucked off twice in the last month. Always lands on that same arm. That pinto of his has got a mean streak."

Melina flushed and drew herself up, finally returning to her tough owner's stance. "Good night, Mr. Dancer."

Colby turned and walked out with Hobbs and Mitts, closing the door behind them. It was moonlight and getting so cold, the chill cut right through their britches.

Hobbs spoke gruffly as they walked down to the horses. "You don't have to go with us, Dancer."

"I seen a wounded cat kill a man once. I'll go."

"Me, too," Mitts said.

"No," Hobbs said, "you're stayin' here to keep an eye on the Jones boys when they get back tomorrow afternoon or evenin', or whenever they show up. I don't trust 'em a lick.

And somebody has to be here with Tommy."

"Why?" Colby asked. "He looks like a healthy young boy. Is she keeping him a prisoner?"

Mitts shook his head. "No, he rides out with the hands. He can saddle his own pony, hunt, throw a rope, and most everything, except he ain't got the size yet."

Mitts walked on ahead, and Hobbs turned to Colby.

"You sure was havin' yourself a look. That's a lady in there."

"But a lot of woman, just the same."

"A mother, *and* another man's wife."

"Don't mean I can't admire what I see."

They mounted and turned their horses toward the bunkhouse where Mitts was waiting in the moonlight. Hobbs tugged at his mustache and turned with a grimace, biting his words.

"Me and Mitts and four hands and Tommy, that's all she's got. The Jones boys are the only gunmen on the place. Now Mr. Ramsey's idea was havin' them here to keep them other hardcases from comin' over from town."

"Where is this Ramsey, anyhow?"

"Well, he had some deal he had to take care of in Butte City. Reckon he's still there. Writes to her now and then."

"No more mail from Indian Station. Last delivery came in Thursday. You got to get over to Pine Ridge to get it now."

"I know, and that's going to be real hard on Mrs. Ramsey. She ain't had a letter for a couple months. Unless the Jones boys bring something back. She don't get a letter pretty soon, old Purvis and his boys might show up on her doorstep."

"What kind of a man is this Ramsey?"

"Big fellah. Handsome, sort of. Talks real educated. Kind of a brooding fellow, like his mind's always somewhere else.

He hired us on in Wyomin' when he picked up his herd, said he had a valley all picked out. Hired the Jones boys and Billy Smith after we moved in here. Right after that, the town turned into a hangout for a bunch of outlaws."

"And I take it she's his second wife?"

"Yeah, married her in Cheyenne last year. His first wife died in childbirth down in New Mexico Territory, leaving him with the boy. Now that Ramsey's away, that Purvis fellow keeps sniffin' around. And the Jones boys are gettin' mighty hard to handle."

The other three hands stayed out for the night with the herd because of the cat, and that night in the bunkhouse, alone with Red, Hobbs and their guest, Mitts played his harmonica for awhile. The redheaded young cowboy was very talkative about the cat, but he had tears in his eyes when he talked about his coon hound and how he'd had to bury it.

"Ain't hardly no dogs left in the whole valley," Red grumbled as he lay back on his bunk. "Except old man Smithers on his farm, but the cat got his dogs a couple weeks ago."

Soon, all were asleep, and Colby lay in the darkness, listening to an owl, wondering about the Jones boys. If they were the Keos, they'd be plenty nervous by now. Colby had difficulty sleeping because he felt he was real close to his targets.

Before dawn, Red, Hobbs and Colby saddled up. Hobbs had tied many ropes on his own saddle, then readied Melina Ramsey's gray mare with a man's saddle. He also showed Colby thirty brood mares, a bay stallion, and a dozen colts and fillies.

"Finest horses in Montana," Hobbs said.

Melina came down from the house wearing heavy clothes with a skirt that fit well over the saddle without revealing her legs above her worn boots. Her wide brimmed hat with a chin strap was pulled down over her black hair, and she carried a Winchester repeater.

Colby watched her as she rode ahead. He thought of Coralee from Lincoln who had run off with a peddler, despite Colby's courting, but she had been nothing like Melina.

Coralee had been sweet and feminine, soft to the touch, but with no loyalty and no decency.

Melina was showing a great deal of courage, trying to keep the ranch together while her husband was gone, but what kind of a man would leave a woman like this in a valley full of outlaws?

Red caught up with Melina and rode at her side.

Hobbs and Colby followed, their gaze scanning the distant forests. They saw far herds of cattle grazing peacefully. By noon, they were across the meadows and at the entrance to Red Rock Canyon, a narrow hollow with walls hundreds of feet high. A small stream came tumbling down over its rocky path and spread out into the meadows.

Tracks of the cat were still in the mud by the creek, and over near the entrance wall, a half-eaten deer was stashed under leaves and branches.

They took a noon break in the shade of the pines just outside the canyon, knowing the wounded cat was in there somewhere. The forested mountains went nearly straight up from the valley floor on each side of the canyon, but the meadows were sweet and green with tall grass, a cattleman's dream.

"It's already got four calves this month," Red was complaining as he leaned against a rock, eyes brimming. "Tore 'em clean apart, dragged 'em off and tried to cover 'em up. Awful."

It was a warm day. Melina removed her hat as she sat on the grass, her long tresses blowing softly in the breeze. Colby could not help but stare at her, and she caught him, her eyes flashing reproach.

"Now," Hobbs said, "I figure that cat's gonna be in the rocks at the end of the canyon, above the waterfall. There are caves up there, but it's too steep for a man to climb without ropes. Maybe two hundred feet up. I figure the cat cuts up through the pines to get there, but this cat is wounded, so we got to make sure it ain't down in the canyon, just waitin' for us."

Melina frowned and twisted a twig in her fingers.

But Colby was gazing at the surrounding terrain. "I can get up around from the side."

"How you gonna do that?" Red asked. "You can't get around that way, not even on foot, unless you're a cat."

"I can ride part way and walk the rest."

"Ain't possible," Red said. "Nobody's ever gotten up there even on foot."

"How would you go?" Hobbs asked.

Colby pointed. "I see a deer trail up there, all the way up along the cliffs."

"More likely mountain goats," Hobbs said. "But I'll wager you'll run square into that cat if you cut up through there."

Melina straightened. "It's too dangerous."

"She's right," Red said.

Melina seemed distressed as she pushed her hair back up inside her hat with the chinstrap snug. "I'll go with you, Mr. Dancer. Hobbs and Red can go up the canyon floor and be ready with rifles if we flush it out."

Hobbs frowned. "Mrs. Ramsey, let one of us go with him. The cat could be waiting in the trees. Now, they don't usually bother people none unless they got young'ns or get cornered.

But you take a wounded cat, and you can't bet on nothin'."

"It's just as dangerous in the canyon," she said. "I'm going with Mr. Dancer, and that's it."

Despite Colby's misgivings, he let her ride behind him, up through the pines to where the steep terrain became impossible for the horses. Here, they had to rein up and dismount, leaving the horses in the trees. They carried their Winchesters and extra cartridge belts.

Some of the trees were lodgepole pines and ponderosa, but mixed in was the strong smell of red cedar. The undergrowth was heavy and tore at their every step.

After they had gone some fifty feet, Colby started to follow another path to the left, but she spoke quickly. "No, let's go straight up."

"Ma'am, you go however you want. I'm following that other trail. I figure them deer know how to get up there."

"I said, we're going straight up."

"And I said, go ahead."

"Mr. Dancer, I don't know what makes you the way you are, but around here, men are a little more cordial to women. But no, not you. You're hostile, and you act like you have nothing inside your head but hard rock. I suspect you'll never change."

"I suspect you're right."

Fury darkened her face, and her eyes were flashing. He turned to the left and started following the winding path. He knew she was following him, but he paid her no mind.

The trail became steeper and more rugged. Insects stirred and lizards scattered. Two bluebirds jumped about in the branches overhead.

Soon they were looking up at a steep, dangerous climb up

the rocky cliffs, and yet they kept going.

Abruptly, he stopped. There was something way off to the left, there in the trees on level ground, a mound of rocks half hidden by brush. Something told him he had to have a look, and her growing hostility convinced him all the more. Besides, Colby was a curious man.

"Keep going," she said.

"That looks like a grave."

"It's not. Now, keep going, straight up, or it'll be dark before we ever find that cat."

There was something in her voice close to terror, and he turned to the left, walking toward it. Sure enough, it was a grave, and the crude cross was purposely hidden under rocks and brush.

He knelt, using his hunting knife to push away the wiry brush, and he rolled back the rocks. He read the name which had been scratched into the wood: Lou Ramsey, 1832–1878.

He stared a long moment as everything about this woman came into focus, and then he heard a shell slamming into the chamber of her Winchester repeater.

CHAPTER FIVE

Slowly turning on one heel, his other knee still on the soft dirt, he looked into the barrel of Melina's gun. Her eyes were smoldering with anger. They were far apart, the barrel of the Winchester just out of his reach.

Carefully, he stood up, but she had the rifle at her shoulder and was aiming dead center at his chest. He spoke quietly, trying to calm her.

"So, that's your secret."

"I'll say I saw a cat, any cat, and when I fired, you got in the way."

"All this to protect the ranch for your son."

"That's right."

"How did your husband die?"

"He thought there was gold up here. He tried riding up that trail. I pleaded with him not to try it, but he never listened to me, and when he got up high, it gave way."

"Does your son know?"

"Yes, of course."

"And Hobbs and the others?"

"No one knows except Tommy. I buried Lou myself."

He was heavy with admiration for her. "And his horse?"

"It fell with him. Broke its leg. I took it way off in the trees and shot it."

"Didn't the men wonder where he was?"

"They were all on a drive."

"And the letters?"

"I write to a friend in Butte City and enclose a letter from him to me. She mails it back as if he wrote it."

"I heard it's been a couple of months."

She flinched. "It'll come."

"So why did he think there was gold up there?"

"He'd seen something on the cliff wall, shining in the sunlight, way up high."

"Well, you won't pull that trigger now."

"And why not?"

"Maybe you would have right off, but you got to talking too long. You have to remember, that's a big mistake."

Melina's face changed many colors. "And if I don't kill you, what then?"

"I'll tell you my secret, and then we'll have to trust each other."

Slowly, she lowered the rifle to waist level, but it was still aimed at his middle. "What do you mean?"

Colby sat down against a stump, hat in hand, running his fingers over his sandy hair. He'd never voluntarily told anyone about his loss, but she could know something about the robbery in Slye through her husband or any of the sinister men in the valley, including Purvis. Maybe it would be worth forcing himself to speak of it, and it might trigger a response.

47

His face was burning, his voice low, his right hand trailing shapes in the dirt with a stick, and he could not look at her as he painfully told her about the bank robbery in Slye and his sister's death.

"Half the county wanted to marry her," he added. "She never said a cross word about anyone in her life."

"Where was your father?" she asked.

"Died when I was small."

"I'm sorry.

Finally he looked up to see a sad look on her face, and he realized she was hearing about Slye for the first time. She was holding the rifle across her arms, her dark hair restless about her face and throat. He got to his feet rather quickly, pulling on his hat, his grim face back to normal.

"Now," he said, "if you tell anyone in Dead Man's Creek, I could be a dead man before I learn the truth. I got no reason to tell your secret, ma'am. You got no reason to tell anyone of mine. Do we have a pact?"

Exhausted, she sat down on a rock, tossing her shining hair from her face. "All right."

He felt awkward to be alone with her. As a married woman, she had been no threat, just a beautiful face to admire. Now that he knew she was a widow, he was afraid of her... and of himself. He tried to sound natural.

"I'm sorry about your husband. But at least you have your son."

"He's not my son. Lou's first wife died in childbirth, leaving Tommy without a mother. Lou was a very intense man. He'd fought for the South, and he never quite got over losing her or the war. He left Tommy with his wife's sister, and he wandered around for nearly seven years. Then a couple of years ago, he came into a lot of money and decided he wanted to build up a ranch for his son."

Colby's mind clicked. "Where did he get the money?"

"New Mexico Territory, an inheritance, he said."

He felt his stomach knot. "What else did he say?"

"I don't remember. When we met in Cheyenne, I was working at the newspaper for my father, but Lou needed a wife to take care of Tommy and that's all. You see, when he was widowed, he near went crazy, and he said he could never be with another woman. You have to respect a man who loves that much."

Realizing what she had said of her private life, she flushed with dark color and started to speak to distract him from her words, but Colby was too quick for her.

"Respect? I'd say he was a fool."

Anger returned to her face, and she wiped away her tears with the back of her hand. "Mr. Dancer, you have a way of making me very angry."

"What's more, why would you marry a man under those conditions?"

She stumbled to her feet, Winchester aimed at him. "I'm starting to rethink this pact."

"You're not going to tell me?"

"It's none of your business. I've already told you more than anyone knows in this valley, except for Tommy. And I've already said enough. So, no, I'm not going to tell you."

"I'll tell you about Coralee."

She hesitated. "Coralee?"

"Only girl I ever wanted to marry, but she ran off with a peddler with holes in his shoes and a squeaky wheel and owing ten dollars for candy at the general store. All because he could dance."

Melina stared at him, incredulous, and when he grinned, she had to laugh, shaking her head, but he persisted.

"So why did you marry Lou Ramsey?"

"I liked him. I thought, in time… but I was wrong."

He sobered. "I'm sorry."

"All I want is to hold onto this ranch for Tommy until he's old enough to take ownership."

"And you'll go on lettin' folks think your husband's alive and in Butte City?"

"Yes."

"They'll catch on, sooner or later, and some of them hardcases will be out here trying to take over. Maybe Purvis will be out in front. You have a lot of cattle and some mighty fine horses in this valley, and that's worth plenty. And I can promise you, the Jones boys won't stop them. They'll join in."

"I hope you're wrong."

They stared at each other for a long moment, and then he removed his hat, running his hand over his hair before pulling it back on tight. He started to walk past her, and then hesitated, looking at her oddly. She was too darned beautiful for her own good.

Unable to stop himself, he reached over and loosened her chinstrap, shoving her hat back so that her raven hair spilled forth in lustrous waves about her throat and shoulders. She was surprised but didn't resist as he twirled a strand around his fingers. Their eyes met, and he couldn't believe he was doing this.

Yet he reveled in the unusual wonders of her face and eyes,

wanting to dig his hands deep into her thick shining hair, and he felt a strange turmoil in his gut. He had never met a woman like her, and it scared the heck out of him.

Uneasy, he turned, walking past her. "I'm going up the trail, and you're staying here."

She hesitated, then nodded. "All right."

"You can cover me from here. And you watch out for the cat, just in case it doubles back."

"Be careful."

He took his Winchester and started up through the pines and boulders, carrying Melina's image in his mind. The dirt and rocks slid under his feet, and he knew she was right. The trail could give way under his weight, the same as it must have for Lou Ramsey.

He kept thinking of her words, that a couple of years ago, Lou Ramsey had come into a lot of money down in New Mexico Territory. It might have no connection, and yet the thought added to his fury, carrying him up the grade.

It took an hour to reach the height he had planned, and there he paused to rest, sweat running down his back and rear. He looked through the trees and down to the grave site, and there was Melina, waving. She looked small as a puppy.

Uneasy, knowing the danger of a wounded cat, he moved out of the trees and along the cliff, the ledge narrowing to three feet in spots, but there was brush just below the edge which gave some feeling of safety.

Running his hand along the sheer wall, he paused, staring at the streaks of yellow, bright and clear in the rock, and further down near his boots, something green in a crease. He shook his head in awe, then continued on his way.

At last, he reached the boulders on the cliff overlooking Red Rock Canyon. It was a two-hundred-foot drop. He peered down at the stream and clusters of cottonwoods and brush, but there was no sign of Red or Hobbs.

A thin stream of water fell from the heights of brush and stone and tumbled down the center wall of the canyon's end, crystal clear over crimson rock, spilling far down to the creek below.

To his left and up some fifty feet, just this side of the waterfall, were two caves, but there were no trails of blood that he could see. If the cat was as badly wounded as Red had claimed, it might not have been able to make it that far.

Kneeling among the rocks, Colby's skin began to crawl as he came around a boulder, looked down at the soft dirt, and saw prints and blood right under his boots.

The hair on the back of his neck stood up, and sweat drenched him. He prayed the cat was not cornered, and that he would see it, wherever it was.

On his heels, rifle ready with shot in chamber, he caught a whiff of blood and hide. He spun about as the great cat came like a ghost out of nowhere, landing on him with such fury, they both crashed backwards toward the edge of the cliff, his Winchester flying into the air.

The cat was nearly two hundred pounds of golden brown death, trying to get at his face and throat as he kept his arms up for protection. He was frantic to get at his belt and his knife or sixgun, but the bloody cat was fighting its last battle. He tried to get at its throat, but each time, its jaws gripped his arm.

They rolled about, Colby's body bloody from gnashing teeth and claws, and now they were on the rim of the cliff, rolling sideways and into space.

They bounced against the wall of stone, and the cat was thrown away from him. Colby clawed at air and passing brush and rocks, alternately clinging, then falling a few feet at a time. He would grab something wiry, but it would break and he would fall again. Two hundred feet of short, jolting breaks.

Then Colby crashed into the arms of a cottonwood by the creek. The limbs bowed, then broke with his weight.

Despite his efforts to grab any part of the tree, he crashed all the way down, scraping himself along the trunk, until he landed on his back in wiry brush that caught him and scratched him all the more. He couldn't believe he wasn't badly hurt.

He fell from the brush and rolled over to the edge of the creek, finally sliding to a halt against some rocks, where he struck his head. He was stunned.

In a daze, he looked up at the two-hundred-foot drop he had somehow survived. Something strange was turning him inside out. He could have died. His life had been suspended in air, in God's hands.

And God had caught him on his way down, dropping him in a cottonwood. The revelation was like ice in Colby's belly.

The Lord could be telling him to rethink his life, and Colby was a religious man. He did not take this lightly.

As he lay there, his flesh torn, Colby continued to stare up at the sheer wall of the cliff. He hadn't felt anything at first, but now pain was setting in like fire in his wounds and agonizing shock in his body. The blow to his head was filling his vision with fog.

A shadow fell across him, and he stared at Hobbs as the amazed foreman knelt down next to him.

"Darndest thing I ever saw. And you're alive."

"Where the heck's my hat?"

As Colby blacked out, Hobbs and Red tried to wash his wounds and clean him off, but they were terrified of infection. Red did retrieve Colby's Stetson, and he volunteered to skin the cat come morning.

It was twilight when Melina came into the canyon with the horses. She dismounted and came hurrying over, then paused to stare down at Colby, who lay unconscious in blankets.

"Don't look, ma'am," Hobbs said.

Melina backed away, remembering her husband's fall. Only this time, the cat had been as dangerous as the drop from the cliff. She touched Colby's brow, finding it cold.

"I can't believe he's alive."

"We ain't moved 'im," Hobbs said. "He hit his head pretty hard. But he's tough."

"We have to help him."

"Right now, the best thing we can do is hold off the infection. We got to keep the wounds clean and dressed. Hot water oughta do it. Come morning, if it's safe to move 'im, we'll build a travois."

They made camp by the creek and built up a good fire in case of a grizzly or another cat. Red sat cross-legged and played his harmonica, the lilting strains of Red River Valley drifting into the cold night air.

Melina huddled in her blankets close to Colby, watching him through the night, remembering his halting words about his loss and his need for vengeance.

"Will he die?" she asked when Hobbs awakened around four in the morning.

Hobbs rose on his elbow. "Maybe, but don't count on it. He's a tough one."

CHAPTER SIX

Red Rock Canyon was cold and damp beyond the campfire Hobbs had built along the creek as first light came.

Melina sat with her arms folded, gazing toward the canyon entrance in time to see two mule deer. One still had its antlers. They drank from the stream, then, graceful and quiet, bounced off toward the valley floor.

She smiled, for they had escaped the cat, at least.

But Colby hadn't. She sobered and moved to kneel beside him, her hand on his brow. He had no fever, thanks to the poultice she had fashioned. She turned to the fire where Hobbs was making coffee and warming up some beans. Red was just getting out of his blankets near the tree, yawning as he stretched.

"I'm hungry."

"Red," Hobbs said, "can't you think of anything but your darned belly?"

"Weren't me."

They turned to see Colby lying with his eyes open. Heavily

bandaged, he couldn't move, but he could turn his head to look at them in somewhat of a surprise.

"Where's my hat?"

"Red has it," Hobbs said, kneeling at his side. "We been afraid to move you. Can you feel your toes? And move your arms and legs?"

Colby gave it a try. "Yeah."

"I checked your limbs while you was out," Hobbs said. "They don't seem broken anywhere."

"My head hurts. And my skin's on fire."

"Mrs. Ramsey put some herbs and moss on the wounds to draw out the poison. We hope."

Colby turned his head the other way and looked up at Melina, who was on her knees at his side. She smiled at him, the early light glistening in her eyes, and he felt better already.

In fact, he felt he was seeing her for the first time. How could he have missed that tiny mole on her cheek? Or the way her nose tipped up slightly at the end. He felt as if something had snapped inside of him, something that opened his eyes.

"It was a terrible fall," she said.

"And the cat?"

"Dead," Hobbs said. "Red's already got the skin stretched. And it's yours."

"We'll give it to Tommy," Colby said.

Hobbs sat on his heels. "I think we can move you. We'll build a travois."

Colby took a long look at Melina. Then he gazed up at the way the cottonwood limbs reached out and upward. He smelled the sweet grass and heard the ripple of the stream, and every sense was alive as if for the first time, reminding him there was more to life and earth than revenge. Peace filled him despite his pain, and he fell asleep.

And as he slept, the Jones boys were just getting up, heavy with exhaustion from their Saturday night. They had bounced around some of the women, gambled away all of their pocket money, and had drunk too much whiskey. Now they were reluctantly getting ready to leave Dead Man's Creek. Before heading out, they stopped to deliver a letter to Purvis in his office.

"From Miles and Mickey," Purvis said, squinting at the poor handwriting. "They're on their way. This letter is old, so they could be here any day now."

"Yeah, well," said Max, puffing on his smoke, "they always scared the heck out of me."

"Don't worry," said Purvis, "I can handle them. Any animal can be herded. Now, was there any mail for Mrs. Ramsey?"

"From Butte City," said Max, handing it over.

Purvis greedily seized the letter and stared at it with great interest.

"This letter's from Mrs. Ramsey, addressed to Lou Ramsey in care of some woman in Butte City. It went there all right, but it came back and it says 'Moved, Address Unknown. Return to Sender'."

"What's that mean?" Max asked.

Purvis smiled. "I got to steam this open."

They followed him over to the iron stove where coffee was boiling in a large enamel pot. Purvis lifted the lid and let the steam rise, holding the envelope over it. In a short while, the seal was broken.

Inside, Purvis saw the return letter addressed to Mrs. Ramsey from Mr. Ramsey. He sat down, his face wrinkled with delight and wonder.

"Boys, she's been writing Ramsey's letters for him. So that tells me either he ran off, or he's dead."

"He wouldn't leave all them cows," Max said. "There's maybe five thousand head out there right now. And a couple hundred head of some fine horse flesh. And no real man would leave a woman like that."

Purvis nodded. "You're right, Max. Ramsey's got to be dead. And she's trying to put this over on all of us."

Skip scratched his head. "Well, I don't get it."

"Never mind," Purvis said. "I do. Now Miles and Mickey ought to be here any day. We got to make a plan, but I can't do it without them."

"Do what?" Skip persisted.

"Well, boys, I'm going to have one of the finest ranches in Montana Territory. We're going to move right in and take it over. And I'm going to marry Melina Ramsey to make it legal."

Max sat down, exhausted from the idea. "So we're just going to ride in and take over?"

"Those hands can't stop us."

Skip made a face. "What about Dancer?"

"Don't worry about him. Miles is faster than Dancer could ever be. And if not, Mickey will just flat out kill him for the fun of it."

"Why do we have to wait?" Max asked. "I'd get Dancer now."

"We need Miles and Mickey. That'll be five of us. And we can hire a few of the men in town when the time comes. There's always some hungry ones, especially after they've been in my gambling hall."

"Yeah," Max said, "we know all about your gambling hall."

"So what about the letter?" Skip asked. "The storekeeper knows we got it."

"I'm gonna reseal it, and you take it to Mrs. Ramsey. I'd sure like to see her face when she realizes her game is up."

Max grinned, hands behind his head as he leaned back in his chair. "Us, gentlemen ranchers."

"I'll be the rancher," Purvis said. "But you boys will get plenty, so don't worry."

"How come you get the woman?" Max demanded.

"Because I'm the boss. And because I've been carrying the two of you and Billy for the past year. You boys spent all your money from Slye, but I've overlooked that. And then you made a mess of that job in Pocket, getting Billy killed for nothing."

Max was still grumbling later when he and Skip returned to the ranch that afternoon. They left the letter with Mitts up at the house but didn't see the boy, and they learned the others were off hunting.

As they ate in the cookhouse out back of the bunkhouse, steam and smoke filling the shack, Max turned to Cookie, talking with his mouth full.

"So if they went after the cat, why aren't they back?"

"It's a wounded cat, and it ain't just waitin' for 'em to play with it. Since it got Red's dog, they ain't got nothin' to tree it with. I figure they could be gone for days."

Skip grimaced and downed his coffee. "We don't need that Colby Dancer around here."

"Maybe not, but Hobbs took a fancy to 'im."

"And Mrs. Ramsey?" Max asked.

"She don't show nothin', but that Dancer's a right handsome

fellow. Mr. Ramsey better hurry up and get back here."

Max turned his hands into fists, his eyes narrowing. "Well, Dancer killed two men in town on Friday night. You can be sure I'm gonna tell her that, first chance I get."

Skip and Max turned in early, still having headaches from their drunken binge, and they were sound asleep when the travois came to the ranch house that evening.

Colby was awake most of the tortuous trip, his whole body aching, and they feared he might be bleeding inside.

He hardly remembered being carried up the stairs at the house, and when he next awakened, it was still dark outside.

He was so hungry, he tried to sit up, his bandages too tight. He winced in pain and lay back, discovering he was lying on a down mattress with satin sheets and under a soft but heavy quilt covering him. A lamp burned on the table, and his gunbelt hung on the wall near it. The furniture was dark wood, and the bed frame was brass.

Through the lace curtains, he could see the glistening leaves of an aspen. He had to be on the second story. The door to the hallway was open, and he could see a lamp on the far wall.

And the boy coming into his room. Colby was really glad to see him, and he managed a smile.

"Hey, you're awake."

"And pretty darn hungry. When's breakfast?"

Tommy grinned. "I'll go tell Mom."

Colby muttered thanks and closed his eyes. He lay quiet, thinking of his own mother, of his four husky brothers, and of his quest, still fruitless.

That fall from the canyon rim had shaken him pretty badly. He could see himself falling every time his eyes closed, his body bouncing everywhere, his legs sprawled, his weight carrying him down toward the canyon floor.

He whispered another prayer of thanks for his survival.

Hearing footsteps, he opened his eyes to see Melina Colby enter the room. Instead of the usual heavy coat, she had a white shawl draped about her and tied in front of her lace-trimmed, high-necked blouse, but it didn't hide as much as she hoped. She looked real good, except that her eyes were red as if she had been crying.

In her hands was a heavy cup of steaming coffee. "If you can get this down, I'll bring you some breakfast."

"Where's Tommy?"

"He went to tell Hobbs and the others. We were very worried about you."

He tried to sit up, but his body hurt so bad, he winced. She set the cup down and bent over him to adjust the pillow behind him. As her dark hair brushed across his face like satin, he caught her left wrist with his right hand and held her there.

She smelled good, like a real woman, and he was caught up in the warmth surrounding her, the softness a man hungers for, even when he's half dead. He had forgotten this need, this want, the way a woman could make a man feel good about himself just by moving a pillow for his comfort.

Her voice was a whisper. "Let me go."

His every movement hurting, he slid his left hand up her right arm to touch her hair, feeling it between his fingers. Funny how a woman's hair was so soft and alive.

Yearning rose from his insides and consumed him. Her face was inches from his, her full lips parted in dismay, but she didn't draw back.

"Kiss me," he said.

"Why should I?"

"Because I got your darned cat."

She was forced to smile, and he pulled her closer while trying to avoid his wounds, the warmth of her surging through him like a prairie fire. Her dark eyes were round and shining in the pale light. When she tried to pull back, he grimaced again in pain, and she relented.

Their lips were so close, he felt her cool breath on his, and he waited, for he would not force it, but he hungered to kiss her. Now she was closing her eyes and she came closer. As her lips pressed to his, he felt his heart grow huge and start to thump like a rabbit's foot.

Their kiss was gentle and slow, though it left him shaken and exhausted like a man who had just survived a stampede. His bitter life had just had a moment of unbridled joy, and it took his breath away. He watched her as she drew back just enough to finish adjusting his pillow. She was dark with color and disconcerted, her hands unsteady.

He couldn't handle what he had just done, and he forced himself to think only of the cup of hot coffee. He let her place it in his hands.

"Mr. Dancer, you've changed."

"Maybe I got scared out there."

She shook her head as she helped him sip the coffee. "I can't believe a man like you is ever afraid. For others, maybe, but not for yourself."

"You give me too much credit."

"Well, then, let's go back to assuming you're a hard-headed, bitter man. And when you're well, you'll go right back to being stubborn, opinionated, a real loner, and a gunfighter with a mission."

He had to grin, but then he sobered. "Just remember, if you tell anyone why I'm here, you could get me killed."

She sat back in the chair. "I gave you my promise, and you gave me yours. I will do anything to keep this ranch for Tommy. And something tells me I'd have a better chance if you were working for me."

"If I can help you, I will, but I can't be tied down. I've got to find those men. And the Jones boys could be Keos, just like Billy. They could have been in Slye when that bank was robbed."

"They work for me. What better way to study them?"

"You've got a point." He sipped the coffee, and it sure was good. "Those herbs and moss you put on me really worked. Where did you learn that?"

"You learn from books when there's no doctor."

He studied her. "You've been crying."

She sniffed back her tears. "The last letter I sent to my friend in Butte City. It just came back, address unknown. There'll be no more letters."

He wanted to tell her not to worry, that he was there, but the thought was strangling. She was right. He was coming back to his old self already, and he wasn't sure he liked it.

It was then that they heard footsteps and soon Hobbs was entering the room, followed by the boy in a nightshirt.

His mother frowned at him. "Tommy, you should be asleep for another hour. You have to do your letters this morning, and I want you to be awake."

"You see that, Mr. Dancer? It's bad enough having a mom

tellin' you what to do, but I got me a mom *and* a teacher, and they're always nagging me."

Colby grinned. "Yeah, they can be a problem."

Melina took Tommy by the hand. "I'll bring up some breakfast as soon as I put this one back to bed."

Tommy looked at the gunbelt and six-guns hanging on the peg near the lamp. "Can I touch 'em, Mom?"

With a sigh, she led him over to the table, and she lifted him enough for him to touch the lowest holster, then set him back down. He turned with a wide smile.

"Boy, Mr. Dancer, I bet you can hit anything."

"Well, I sure hit that cottonwood."

"I bet that was really somethin'. I bet it was real exciting, like riding a waterfall or somethin'."

"Or something," Colby said.

When the mother and son were gone, Hobbs pushed his hat back and pulled up a chair to chat with him about the cat and the ranch. He told Colby the Jones boys were back and lying around the bunkhouse as usual.

"They ain't good for nothin'. But they couldn't wait to tell Mrs. Ramsey you'd killed two men on Friday night."

"It was a fair fight. They came after me. Rustlers I'd been hunting down in Wyoming. Reckon they thought I'd back-shoot them."

"You goin' to work for us?"

"Mrs. Ramsey offered me a job, but I don't know."

"I'd sure like to see you run off the Jones boys."

"Right now they're between her and the town. If I run them off and then I leave, what then?"

"Maybe Mr. Ramsey will be back before there's trouble."

"Yeah, what about this Ramsey? I understand he came into a lot of money down in New Mexico Territory a couple years ago. You know anything about that?"

"Nope."

"Well then, what do you know about Purvis?"

"Smooth-talking dude. Spent a lot of money settin' himself up, and he's probably tripled it by now. All them bad ones comin' in lookin' for a hideout and stayin' until they run out of money. Some folks in town wrote to the U.S. Marshal, twice, but nobody's ever come. They just figure the letters never got out."

"How about Jackson? He claims to have made his poke hunting for the railroad."

"Yeah, that's true all right. Some of them Reb outlaws don't like him much, but he's the only smithy, and he makes a good living."

"These Jones boys, do they have a lot of money to throw around?"

"When they first come to the valley, they sure enough did. But if they got any left, I figure they're spendin' it all in Purvis's place. They go every Saturday."

"They went down to Wyoming with Billy Keo to deliver that stallion. Makes me wonder if Skip and Max are really Keos."

"Well, when they come here, they said they was all cousins, and they looked alike. But I don't reckon they're gonna admit anything."

They paused as Melina brought a bowl of hot, thick oatmeal, and she sat next to Colby, offering him a spoonful.

"Mush? I was looking for bacon and eggs."

"Eggs come from the Smithers farm, but I don't have any right now. Now eat."

Hobbs was grinning. "She's the boss."

She shoved a spoonful into Colby's mouth. "I've asked Hobbs to sleep downstairs while you're here."

"Yeah, can you imagine that, Dancer? Me, a chaperon. And here you are in such bad shape, you can hardly move. Nobody's got to worry about you any." Hobbs chuckled with a twinkle in his eye. "Maybe she oughta be worryin' about me, huh?"

Melina shook her head. "You're like a grandfather to me, Mr. Hobbs. And a great grandfather to Tommy."

Hobbs was misty eyed. "I was married once. Had two sons. They was both killed in the War Between the States. Now I got nobody anywhere except here."

"Mr. Hobbs," she said, her hand on his arm, "I'm very glad you are here. And so is Tommy."

Later that day, Colby was still in pain. Mitts and Red had stopped by on their way to the herd. Then Hobbs came to change his bandages, and Colby winced at the sight of the torn flesh on his arms and chest, but it was going to heal sooner or later. There seemed to be no infection.

Toward evening, Colby insisted Hobbs bring him his britches and help him get his clothes on, his shirt pulled over to loosely cover the bandages. It was still painful, but he couldn't stay in bed like a dead man. His coat was put over his shoulders for warmth, and he insisted on wearing his gunbelt.

Out on the porch, Hobbs showed him the cougar's hide stretched between two aspens. The old cowhand was really impressed with the cat.

"More than two hundred pounds, I'll bet."

"Sure felt like it."

"You know, Colby, that was nigh on to a miracle. How you

came out alive, we'll never know, but it seems like the good Lord's got somethin' for you to do. Now, it might be a sight more than killin' Keos."

Colby shrugged, his own thoughts similar.

That evening, Colby was able to sit in one of the leather chairs by the fire. Tommy, left arm still in a sling, was sitting near his feet. Hobbs sat telling stories of the cattle trail while Colby couldn't take his eyes off of Melina. She seemed more shy and careful around him, and he was a bit uneasy himself.

All the while, he knew the Jones boys were here on the ranch, two men who could have been in the holdup that killed his sister. And he knew he had to protect Melina, especially now that the letters from Butte City had stopped. Maybe it would all work out at the same time.

As Colby stared into the fire and listened to Hobbs, Melina marched Tommy upstairs and waited until he was in bed, the lamp shining on his yellow hair.

"Mom, do you like Mr. Dancer?"

"Well, Tommy, he's a gunfighter, and we don't know him very well."

"He hunted rustlers. He got the bad guys."

She sat on the edge of the bed. "I don't want you to get too fond of him. He may not be around long."

"He come here lookin' for somebody, didn't he? There's gonna be a big fight, huh?"

She drew the covers up to his chin. "You go to sleep, young man."

"I really like him, Mom. Better than Pa."

Her face tightened. "What a terrible thing to say."

"Pa never liked me. He was crazy about my mother and

blamed me for her dyin', on account of me bein' born. That's why I was stayin' with my aunt until he met you. I guess that's right after he got all that money and figured he'd have a big ranch up here. But it wasn't on my account."

"Tommy—"

"If he hadn't met you, I'd never have seen him again. He never hugged or kissed me. Never played with me or took me hunting or fishing. He just didn't like me, Mom."

Tears came to her eyes. "Tommy, he loved you, but he was a man who was hurting really bad."

"Mr. Dancer hurts real bad, I can tell, but he's nice to me. I think he likes me."

"Of course, he likes you."

"Mom, if you married Mr. Dancer, nobody could hurt us."

"Tommy—"

"Think about it, Mom."

"Mr. Dancer's life could be very short, Tommy. Now I want you to go to sleep."

Tears on her cheeks, she kissed him and left the room.

In the morning, they were all having a late breakfast when there was a pounding at the door.

CHAPTER SEVEN

Hobbs went to answer the door, and the man who walked in was dressed like a dandy in a Sunday suit.

It was Purvis, his pale hair slicked back, a big foolish smile on his face, and his small hat in hand. He bowed to Melina, smiled at an annoyed Tommy, and merely nodded at Colby and Hobbs.

Melina smiled politely. "Mr. Purvis. Please join us."

She stood up to give him her chair, but he shook his head. "No, I can bring up that bench. The Jones boys told me about the cougar that nearly finished Mr. Dancer. By the look of its hide out there, it must have weighed two hundred pounds."

"I get to hang it in my room," Tommy said.

Melina served Purvis some bacon and beans while Hobbs reluctantly related the full story of the hunt. Purvis pretended to be impressed, and he ate with excellent manners, but he was annoyed with Tommy's bragging.

"Mr. Dancer fell two hundred feet and he hardly got hurt. Why, he sprouted wings or somethin'. But that ole cat couldn't take it one bit."

Listening to the conversation, Colby kept thinking about the educated man with gray eyes, like Purvis, who had orchestrated the Slye robbery. A man with a thin nose, just like Purvis.

But Colby was also getting annoyed with Purvis's attention to Melina. He was grim as Purvis chortled.

"Mrs. Ramsey, I brought my new buggy, and I hope you'll let me take you for a ride in it. I have a fine, high-stepping black in harness."

"She's busy," Tommy said, nose wrinkling. "She has to take care of Mr. Dancer."

Purvis smiled smoothly. "It's good of you to protect your mother, Tommy. Perhaps you would like to ride with us."

Melina brought more coffee. "I'm sorry, Mr. Purvis, but I'm baking bread today, and Tommy will be helping me. But I'll be happy to come outside and look at your new rig before you leave. I'm sure you'll want to be home by dark."

And so it was that Melina later walked outside into the sunlight, Tommy at her heels, to follow Purvis to his buggy and the nervous black. The rig had a high, fringed top and a wide, black cushioned seat. The wheels were tall and thin.

Melina inspected it. "It's very fancy, Mr. Purvis."

"Are you sure you can't come for a ride?"

"She already said no," Tommy said. "And we have to look after Mr. Dancer."

"Perhaps you don't know Colby Dancer killed two men in a gunfight last Friday night. I was very surprised to see him in your house, Mrs. Ramsey. He's a cold-blooded killer."

"I don't believe you," Tommy said. "If he killed two men, it was a fair fight, right, Mom?"

Melina brushed her hair from her face. "If it was two against one, it must have been fair, don't you think, Mr. Purvis?"

"May I speak with you alone?"

Melina hesitated, then nodded. "Go back into the house, Tommy."

"Aw, Mom."

Melina insisted, and the boy walked back to the house, kicking every rock he could find on the way. At the porch, he paused, then sat down on the steps to watch, out of earshot, but with a grim look on his face.

Purvis, hat in hand, turned to Melina. "Mrs. Ramsey, it may be unseemly, but I have to speak of what's in my heart. Now it could be your husband never returns, and then what? You need a man to look after you and the boy."

"My husband will be back soon."

"But you don't know for sure. And there's been no letter for two months."

Melina stiffened and folded her arms in the rising wind, her breath tight, praying he hadn't seen the returned letter, that he hadn't figured it out, and yet, there was something new and dangerous in his smile. She had to remain calm.

"It was nice of you to visit, Mr. Purvis. Good day."

"How a man like Ramsey ever got you, I'll never know."

"What do you mean, a man like—"

"I'm sorry. I misspoke."

"I think you had better explain yourself."

Purvis held his hat to his chest. "It grieves me to tell you this, but Lou Ramsey was an outlaw ever since the War. He never surrendered to the Union, just like a lot of Rebs. But after a while, he and his gang stopped fighting the Union, and started robbing and killing anyone who got in their way."

Melina caught her breath, then shook her head. "No, that's not true. He had a ranch in New Mexico Territory."

"That's what he said, but his wife died in childbirth near Mesilla, all because he was off on a raid instead of there to help her. He nearly went crazy, screaming in his sleep. And he's lived with the guilt ever since."

"And how do you know all this?"

Purvis frowned. "I'm sorry to say that for some time, I dealt in stolen goods, which Lou Ramsey brought to me from his raids. I finally stopped out of conscience. But when he bought a big herd and came up here, I knew I could open my businesses south of the bridge with no interference. Why else do you think he never sent for the law when all those wanted men started coming into my side of town?"

"I don't believe you."

"I make a lot of money, Mrs. Ramsey. That's what it's all about. At least you know where I stand and what I've been, and I'll never lie to you like Ramsey did. In fact, I'm a much better man for you. At least I'm not a killer."

"I think you've said quite enough, Mr. Purvis."

He gazed at her intensely. "Seeing the wind in your hair, the way you look, a man couldn't ask for much more. I know you're a real woman just waiting for the right man. And I'm that man, Mrs. Ramsey."

"Good day, Mr. Purvis. And you had best not be spreading those lies about Mr. Ramsey."

"Oh, it's between you and me, because I intend to take his place."

"I want you to leave, right now, Mr. Purvis, and I don't want you to ever come back."

"Oh, I'll be back, and nobody will stop me."

He smiled, eyes narrowed and gleaming. Then he bowed slightly, donned his hat, and climbed into the buggy. Melina stood back as he turned it around, then reined to a halt to look her over once more.

"No other man is going to have you, Melina. You belong to me. And don't you forget it."

She caught her breath at the dark, crazy look in his eyes. His mouth was tight and sinister. His skin seemed to change to an orange tint. There were strange movements of his fingers as he moved his hat back and forth. He seemed to be hunched over as if to leap from the buggy. His demeanor caused her to stand as tall as she could in defiance.

Purvis tipped his hat and drove away, leaving her to wrap her arms more tightly about herself, trying to stop her chills. She realized now she was shivering down to her boots as if she had fallen in Dead Man's Creek in the middle of winter.

She saw him drive down the hill and pull up by the bunkhouse where the Jones boys were standing. Shaken and queasy, she turned and walked back to the house where Tommy was waiting on the steps. The boy stood up, anxious.

"Mom, you look scared."

"No, I'm all right, Tommy."

But when they went inside, she turned into the other room and hurried up the stairs, wanting to be alone to compose herself. As she sat on the bed, she reached for the Winchester repeater she kept by the post, and she checked the load in the chamber, determined to protect herself, the boy, and the ranch. All the while, tears trickled down her face.

Meanwhile, Purvis was talking to the Jones boys, his buggy

stopped near the bunkhouse. He acted as if he owned the world in that new rig, but the Jones boys were not impressed.

"You're wasting your time, Purvis," Skip said.

"Yeah," Max agreed. "She'd rather have me."

"You stay away from her, both of you."

"Yeah, well," Max said, "what about Dancer making hisself at home in there, shinin' up to her? I'd like to blow his head off."

"Yeah," Skip said. "Why wait for Miles and Mickey? I'm gettin' sick of Dancer."

Purvis straightened and shifted his weight on the buggy seat. "Well, if you really are in a hurry, it's worth $500 to the man who kills him."

Skip smiled. "No matter how it's done?"

"That's right. But don't let anyone see you. I want you boys to be able to stay out here and look after my interests until Miles and Mickey get here. Just don't take any chances. I'll need you when the time comes."

Max pushed his hat back, throwing away his smoke. "And what makes you the big he-bull around here?"

Annoyed, Purvis shifted his weight. "You're mighty ungrateful. I've been carrying the both of you for a long time. I expect some loyalty in return."

As Max and Skip argued in hushed voices by the bunkhouse, a visitor was arriving in the town of Dead Man's Creek.

The preacher rode up to Jackson's livery barn on the north side of the creek. Jackson was sweating heavily as he worked iron on the fire, and he hardly glanced at the stranger.

"Son, they call me Preacher."

"Jackson."

"You got a place for me to sleep, Mr. Jackson?"

"Up in the loft."

The preacher swung down from the saddle and moved closer. "I'm looking for all the wicked men in town. I plan to smite them with the sword of God. Some are called Keos. You know them?"

Jackson paused and looked into the man's searing dark gray eyes. "Lot of men south of the creek using most any name they choose. Maybe you'll find 'em down there."

"You're a good man, Mr. Jackson."

"How do you know that?"

"Because you look right into my eyes and don't turn away. You're only the second man in this territory could do that. The other was called Colby Dancer. Do you know where he is?"

"Nope."

"Has he been to town?"

"Yep."

"But you don't know where he is?"

"Nope."

"I've heard he hunted rustlers down on the Powder River. Why do you think he's here in a place like this?"

"I don't know. Maybe he's still hunting rustlers. Or preachers."

The preacher studied him a long moment, then pushed his hat back and grinned. "I like you, Mr. Jackson."

"Glad to hear it."

"What would it cost me to find out where Colby Dancer is?"

Jackson shrugged. "I don't know anything."

"Loyalty? I like that in a man."

The preacher led his horse into the barn, leaving Jackson to stare after him, and later, he walked down the street and across the bridge as Jackson watched, shaking his head.

Out at the Rockin' R, Colby Dancer was grimacing in pain as Hobbs pealed off the bandages.

"Hold on, son. It's stickin' to your skin."

Colby knew that Melina and Tommy were watching, and he was as brave as possible. Hobbs was cleaning him off with alcohol, which cooled him and eased the pain of his wounds.

"You're healin' up right fine, son. I think you can leave off the bandages to give it a chance. But you use that there bear grease if it ever starts itching."

Colby breathed easier as Hobbs helped him pull his shirt back on, and he felt better already. His aching body was recovering from the trauma, and there was no evidence of internal bleeding. In fact, he would soon be ready to take up his quest.

But later that evening with Tommy at his side, reading to him from a three-year-old, October, 1876, *St. Louis Globe-Democrat*, and Melina sitting near the fire as she stitched up a shirt, he was a contented man. Tommy held up the newspaper to the light of the nearby lamp.

"'...to rid the country of the grasshopper pest.' Mr. Dancer, what's a grasshopper?"

"A big bug. Jumps around the corn field."

"It says they're gonna ditch and burn them. Yuck." Tommy read the article, then skipped elsewhere. "Here, listen to this. 'Negroes hunted like partridges in Claiborne County.' It says there are riots in Jackson, Mississippi. Why would they do that, Mr. Dancer?"

"The War's never going to be over for anyone who lived through it."

"Mr. Jackson in town, why don't they hunt him like they're doing down in Mississippi?"

"First of all, they need him—he's the only smithy in town. And second, he'd blow their heads off with that old buffalo gun of his."

Tommy grinned and held up the paper again. "Here, it says 'The Delaware and Hudson Canal will sell 100,000 tons of Lackawanna coal at auction.' How much coal is that, Mr. Dancer?"

"Bigger than this house."

"You know everything, don't you, Mr. Dancer? Hey, look, it says the 'Turkish Consul and his wife assassinated at Tiflis.' Where's that, Mr. Dancer?"

Melina spoke up quickly. "Tommy, you've read that newspaper a hundred times in the last year. And you know that Tiflis is in Asiatic Russia, just like it says."

"But I want to read to Mr. Dancer some more."

"It's time for bed. Now, run along, and I'll be up soon."

Reluctant, the boy folded the newspaper. "I'll read you some more tomorrow, Mr. Dancer."

When Tommy had gone into the other room and up the stairs, Colby grinned at Melina. "Thanks."

She glanced at the sleeping Hobbs, then leaned forward, her voice low. "I'm worried. Tommy is fascinated by you, and it's going to cause him a lot of pain if you're killed, or if you turn out to be one huge lie."

"Ma'am, if anyone kills me, I'm going to be just as upset as Tommy."

She stared at him a long moment, then leaned back, her small nose wrinkling. "And what if you turn out to be one big lie?"

"Everything I've told you is the truth. And there's something else you ought to know. When I was climbing up after that cat, I saw color."

"What do you mean, color?"

"In the wall along the high ledge, before I got over to where the cat was. There's streaks of gold up there. Maybe silver. I didn't have time to scrape it out, but it seems your husband did see something after all."

She wrapped her arms about herself, staring at him. "If that's true, I'll thank you to keep it to yourself. I don't need this place crawling with prospectors."

"I got no reason to tell anyone."

"Well, there's something you can tell me. Why would an obviously educated man spend his time chasing rustlers in the first place?"

"I was good at it. Why does a handsome woman marry a near stranger?"

Her face darkened and she gripped the thread, snapping it from the shirt in her hands. They studied each other as the fire spit and crackled and as Hobbs snored softly.

"He was the first man to interest me."

"Or who didn't know the truth."

She half rose from the chair. "What are you implying?"

"Long black hair, high cheek bones, graceful as a cat. Moss and herbs on a wound. That's you. And your ancestors. Sioux or Cheyenne?"

CHAPTER EIGHT

She glanced quickly at Hobbs, then stood up and walked over to glare down at Colby in the firelight, her voice wavering. "You're making a mistake, Mr. Dancer."

He reached to seize her hand, grasping it in his big fingers. "It don't matter where you came from, Mrs. Ramsey. You're the best-looking woman in the whole country."

Pulling her hand away, she stood a little taller. "If you ever tell anyone what you've implied here tonight, I will kill you."

"Because you're ashamed? Or to save the ranch?"

"Mr. Dancer, you are taking a lot of liberties. I'll thank you to keep your thoughts to yourself."

As she strutted past, he stood up and reached out to catch her left arm with his right hand, spinning her about so that her hair flew in all directions. She lost her balance and tipped away from him, but he held her steady, his fingers tight above her elbow.

"If I wasn't a wounded man—"

She drew herself up, trying to pull free of his grip. "You would do nothing, Mr. Dancer. You are just a gunfighter, and all we need around here is those fancy six-guns. I have no interest in you whatsoever."

He pulled her closer. "That why you kissed me?"

"That was a thank you for a man who had been hurt."

"Didn't taste like it."

She jerked free, dark eyes flashing and her chin in the air. "When you came here, you were a walking animal. Now you're trying to be human, and it doesn't work, Mr. Dancer. You will never be anything more than a pair of six-guns. Goodnight."

She spun on her heel and stormed into the other room and up the stairs. This was a woman any man would fight for, but Colby was too mixed up inside, too long on the vengeance trail, too much of a coward around her.

He spent a sleepless night, and at first light, he was out walking among the aspens. He was wearing his gunbelt and tugging at his hat, feeling the chill under his coat, the scars from his wounds as sensitive as his lonely heart.

He could smell coffee down at the cook shack, and he wandered down that way as the first rays of the sun danced on the wet grass. The dark green mountains rose in the distance like protective walls around the valley, shielding bears and cougars and sending elk and deer down to the meadows. A man could get used to this, he thought.

A young man came out of the bunkhouse and stretched before pulling on his hat. He was wearing a fancy gunbelt and decorated boots. Pausing to look at Colby in the first rays of the sun, he frowned.

"So you're that fancy gun she's lookin' after."

"Colby Dancer. And you'd be one of the Jones boys."

"That's right. Skip Jones. My brother Max is already at

breakfast, and if you ain't afraid, maybe you can join us. We got to ride out to the herd today."

"I'm surprised you do any work around here."

"What kind of a crack is that?"

"Well, the others are always out with the cattle or working the horses, and the two of you seem to spend most of your time in town with gambling and painted women."

Skip studied him. "Oh, yeah?"

"I'll pass on breakfast."

"Oh, yeah?"

"The two of you are too dangerous for me."

"Oh, yeah?"

"I'm quaking in my boots."

"*Oh, yeah?*"

Abruptly, Max Jones poked his head out of the cookhouse. "Hey, Skip, aren't you—well, if it isn't the fancy Mr. Dancer."

Colby studied both of them as they looked him over. He felt as if he had worms in his gut. These men could be Keos, and they could have been at the robbery in Slye, but he had no proof.

Colby turned and walked back up the slope toward the house. Skip played with the handle of his sixgun, his mouth twisting and eyes narrowing. Angry, he hurried back into the cookhouse with Max.

Pausing in the aspens to look back down the slope, Colby grimaced. Two years, and his fury was still buried in his middle like a hot rock.

Later that morning, Mitts and Colby went riding off through the valley. Tommy had begged to go, but Melina refused him because his arm was still painful enough to stay in the sling.

Although Colby still hurt from his healing wounds, he was

glad to be in the saddle. The smell of his horse's sweat, the creak of good leather, the wind in his face, it made a man feel alive and comfortable.

He had brought along his saddlebags and bedroll, figuring on heading back to town, but he was in no hurry to leave this breathtaking land.

They joined some of the herd where they met with the other hands, seasoned trail drivers. They saw the Jones boys on a far ridge circling some of the cows and calves.

"Don't like them much," Mitts said. "They can't do hardly anything with cattle. They're only out here today to count, and I have to check it myself when they's all done. When we start brandin', maybe they can use an iron, but I doubt it. Unless it's a runnin' iron."

Colby leaned on the horn. "Well, I'm heading for town. Anything you want?"

"Some of that striped candy, maybe." Mitts tossed him a coin. "For Tommy."

"What that boy needs is a dog."

"Ain't hardly any in the valley right now. Them fellahs in town, they got no need for dogs. And the cat killed the two old ones Smithers had, but left a couple of pups he's been nursin'. His place is on the way back to town, over yonder."

"Smithers?"

"You can't miss it. Only cornfield in the valley. You'll see a black butte near his place. Just opposite Ramsey's gate."

"Maybe I'll stop there on the way back."

"No way he's gonna sell you them pups."

"Listen, Mitts, you keep an eye on Mrs. Ramsey while I'm gone," and Mitts nodded.

Colby headed toward town later that afternoon. He followed the wagon road this time, taking it leisurely, enjoying the sparkling creek and the cottonwoods.

The valley rolled in all directions, green and bright in the sunlight. As twilight came on, he was passing the big arch that signalled the Rockin R.

Seeing a woodpecker on a high limb, he had reined up to get a look, and he managed to lean back just as a bullet creased the right side of his head. He jerked from the pain and spun his sorrel around but saw nothing as another bullet slammed past him and into the tree. The shots were coming from the cover across the creek.

Pulling his Winchester and dropping from the saddle, Colby moved behind the rocks and brush. He waited, watching for movement as his horse nervously drifted away.

He stuck his hat on the end of his rifle and raised it slowly. A bullet slammed through it, spinning it, and he lowered his Stetson, grimly noting the hole in the crown. Now he knew where they were. Across the way in the rocks near a dead cottonwood with bare limbs.

He settled into the wiry brush and rested against a rock as blood trickled down near his right ear. He pulled off his bandanna and wiped some of it away. It was going to be dark soon, and he wondered just how bad they wanted him.

Once in awhile, a bullet would spit off the rocks around him. They were letting him know they were waiting him out, and they didn't plan on leaving until he was dead. He figured there were two of them and their names were likely Skip and Max.

Night fell, and Colby began to inch his way through the rocks on his belly. Just before he reached the creek bank, he saw movement over by the bare cottonwood. He lifted his sixgun and fired.

There was a yelp, then cussing, followed by abrupt silence. Suddenly, two riders were galloping off in the darkness, heading down the other side of the creek toward town. They sure looked like the Jones boys, but he couldn't swear by it.

Colby jumped up with his Winchester, but they were gone.

He soaked his bandanna in the cold creek and washed the crease on the side of his head, which was aching. His sorrel had come wandering back, and he decided to camp for the night.

Before daylight, he headed for town, wondering if the Jones boys were going to be hiding and waiting for him. If they were Keos like Billy, how many others of the gang were in the valley?

Riding up the wagon road with the town starting to show in the early morning light, he checked his Colts by habit, even though he had already done so in camp.

The south side of town looked peaceful enough, but there was no sign of life. Even the hotel was dark and silent. He rode across the bridge to see smoke curling from Jackson's forge. When he reached the smithy, Jackson paused to look up with a grin as he wiped the sweat from his brow.

"So you're still alive."

Colby leaned on the horn and pushed his hat back. "The Jones boys in town?"

"Ain't seen 'em."

"Two men took a shot at me by the creek yesterday. I winged one of them, I think."

"Well, if the Jones boys are in town, they're over at Purvis's hotel of joy. If the preacher didn't talk 'em out of it. He's been spoutin' the word of God all over that part of town. Wonder they ain't shot him yet. He's over at the Red Feather right now. You buy me a cup of coffee, we'll see if he knows anything."

They left the sorrel at the livery and walked across the street to the saloon. Inside, the only customer was the preacher, minus his white collar, sitting at a table by the back wall. He beckoned to them to join him as the fat, round cook picked up his empty plate.

There was something about the preacher that irritated Colby, but he couldn't quite put his finger on it. Unless it was that the man was a fake.

Leaning back as they sat down and ordered coffee, the preacher removed his hat and ran his fingers over his gray hair as he smiled at Colby, his dark, gleaming eyes more friendly.

"Mr. Dancer, I prayed for you, just as you asked."

"Thanks. Maybe that's why I'm still alive. You do any praying for Jackson here?"

"Mr. Jackson is a hard-working, honest man, and in the eyes of the Lord, that's a prayer in itself."

Jackson grunted. "How do you know I'm honest?"

The preacher's thin nose twitched. "I know all about you and your days with the Union Pacific. But I don't know Mr. Dancer, except by reputation."

The cook brought them coffee, and Colby sipped it, then leaned back to study the preacher. "You don't look like any preacher I ever knew. They don't pray, you send them to the devil with your Colt?"

"Son, every man prays whether he knows it or not, and when he's dying, his tongue loosens up mighty fast."

"What church are you with?"

The preacher studied him a long moment. "My son, you have no faith. God's church is everywhere."

"I'll wager your agenda's a little bit different than His."

"You're trying my patience, son."

Jackson looked from one to the other. "Something's going on here that I want no part of. I'll see you later."

With the smithy gone, the preacher fingered his coffee cup and then leaned forward on his elbows, his eyes narrowed to slits. "I know about your sister."

Colby tensed, one hand gripping the table's edge. "How do you know? Were you there?"

"No, I wasn't. But I know all about you, Colby Dancer, and I know why you're here. The sheriff of Pocket told me about you and Billy Keo. I cut trail to catch up with you."

"So, you're no preacher."

"We're all preachers, son." And the man looked toward the bar, but there was no sign of the cook. Still, he spoke more softly. "You're loco to have come here alone. There's at least fifty men south of the bridge that would love to string you up."

"Something tells me I'm not alone."

The preacher worked his wide mouth. "God is always with us, son."

"I figure the Jones boys are Keos, but they don't count for much. I'm really looking for Mickey and Miles. It was Mickey who pulled the trigger that got my sister. Kansas Grange used to be connected with them, but I can't prove anything or even find him. Now, who are you looking for?"

"Maybe all of them."

"Are you a bounty hunter? And don't tell me every man's a bounty hunter."

The preacher chuckled, lifting his cup. "The marshal of Slye gave me a lot of information about you."

"So you been dogging my trail?"

CHAPTER NINE

For a moment, the preacher concentrated on his cup, and he downed his coffee before answering, his voice low in the empty saloon.

"I'm afraid I have."

"Why?"

"Let's just say we're hunting the same men."

"Well, what have you found out?"

"Nothing so far, but I have made a lot of folks nervous."

Colby thought he could speak freely with the preacher. He told him about Purvis, the Jones boys, the Rockin' R, and the cat that nearly killed him. But he didn't mention Ramsey's grave.

"This Ramsey," the preacher said. "You say he came into a lot of money in New Mexico Territory about two years ago. I'd sure like to talk to him."

"So would I. But let's not forget, Purvis came about the same time with his own bundle of cash, and he set himself up here with no trouble."

"I've heard about this Purvis, but he was busy at his wretched hotel when I went over there last night. What does he look like?"

"Gray eyes, thin nose, husky fellow. Light brown hair."

The preacher frowned. "Well, now, that's pretty close to the description of a Keo I used to know. His first name was also Purvis. Care to walk over with me?"

"Yeah, sure."

The two men walked out into the sunlight. Only a few people were stirring around the town. Everyone here was very careful about being outdoors.

As they crossed the bridge, the preacher frowned. "Those people on the north side, they're prisoners in their own town. Afraid of these heathen."

"You know, we could be walking into trouble. Can you hit anything with that Colt of yours?"

"Son, you see that cottonwood way over there? I could draw your name on it in no time at all."

"That's a hundred yards."

"The Lord doesn't like braggarts, but I will show you one of these days."

Colby didn't really believe him because a sixgun was only accurate to about seventy five yards. They moved down the street toward the Silver Dollar on their left. Beyond it, they could see the shacks and tents with some women walking around half dressed.

"Abomination," the preacher said.

As they entered the Silver Dollar, they saw two men playing cards at a corner table, both with beards and beady eyes and suspicion in their gaze. There was no one else in the saloon except Purvis, who was busy behind the bar working on some books.

Colby and the preacher walked up to the bar.

Annoyed at being bothered, Purvis looked up and glared at Colby. Then he looked at the preacher and he turned white, all color draining from his face, his hands gripping the book, his voice tight.

"What are you doing here?"

"All the forsaken come to this place, don't they?"

"I thought you were dead."

The preacher put both hands on the bar, his fingers tapping gently. "Want to make it a fact?"

"I'm not drawing on you, Kansas."

Colby felt a knot in his middle then, and he turned to stare at the preacher, wondering if it could be true, but not sure. He watched the two men argue back and forth.

"Purvis, is it? Ashamed of your last name?"

"Listen to me, Kansas. There's no room for you here."

"Maybe I'll make room."

"There's at least fifty men in my town can make short work of you."

"I'm only interested in you and your kin."

Purvis wiped his face with a bar towel, but his color didn't return. "You start trouble, this whole town will blow wide open."

"Could be you came into a little money a couple years ago, down in Slye, New Mexico Territory."

"Never been there."

The preacher smiled thinly. "I suspect Skip and Max will have a different story to tell."

"I've got no time for you," Purvis said as the barkeep walked into the room. "And I'd thank you to leave. Having Kansas Grange around would scare off half my customers."

With that, Purvis turned and walked into a back room, slamming the door behind him. The preacher turned and walked out, Colby on his heels with his mouth wide open.

In the bright sunlight, they walked along the street toward the bridge, and Colby was grim.

"He called you Kansas Grange."

"He could be mistaken."

"I got a feeling there's a lot more about you I had better find out, and I'm not a patient man."

"That I know from the marshal in Slye."

"Who the heck are you, preacher?"

"Let's head out to the Rockin' R. I want to meet the Jones boys."

"I don't want you out there. You cause trouble, and Mrs. Ramsey and the boy could get hurt."

But there was no stopping Kansas Grange, and later that afternoon, they headed west on the wagon road, bedrolls tied over their saddlebags behind the cantles.

"We have to make a stop at Smithers's farm," Colby said. "Got to buy a pup for the boy."

"You getting involved there, son?"

"Stop calling me son. I'm no kin to the likes of you."

"Maybe you're lucky."

"I don't know whether to call you preacher or Kansas."

"Don't matter now. Purvis blew my cover."

"And what about Purvis? Who is he?"

"He's one of the Keos. Billy's uncle, Purvis Keo."

"So he was in on it."

"We don't know that for sure. But I suspect all of 'em were Keos that day in Slye. They always ran in a pack."

Colby shifted his weight in the saddle, glancing toward the Black Butte. They turned south to Smithers's farm, nestled against the mountain range with some straggly fruit trees, a cornfield, henhouse, and some pigs.

"Must be a mighty popular man around here," Kansas said.

The farmhouse was single story, surrounded by sheds and pens and corrals. As they reined up, they could hear the snorting hogs, which made their horses nervous.

Kansas only gave his first name, and the Smithers had never heard of Colby. It was a warm noon as the couple invited them inside to have a meal of bacon and eggs. The visitors stuffed themselves.

Mrs. Smithers was thin from hard work, her face lined and her clothes faded, but she was always smiling and touching her gray hair, tied back in a bun. Her husband was also thin and worn, his hair near gone and his long face cut by a wide smile.

As the three men went outside, Colby turned to the farmer. "I hear you have a couple of pups."

"Yeah, sure, come on."

Back of a shed in a dog house, surrounded by heavy wire, were two black and white pups with white faces, large brown eyes and floppy ears.

"Border collies," Smithers said. "Lost their ma and pa to that cat a couple weeks ago."

"Cat's dead," Colby said.

"That a fact? How so?"

"I tangled with it in Red Rock Canyon, up on the cliff. We both fell, but I landed in a tree. The cat hit the rocks and was killed right off. Hide's out at the Ramsey place."

Smithers stared at him. "Mr. Dancer, you're full of surprises. Here, I'll let you play with the pups."

The farmer opened the gate, and Colby knelt as the two male pups came jumping out of the little house. The first was big and fluffy, full of fight and bounce. The second was a runt, walking crooked toward him.

"How much for the runt?"

"They ain't for sale," Smithers said.

"Even for the Ramsey boy?"

Smithers made a face. "I said, they ain't for sale."

"Even for the price of a dead cat?"

"You ain't playin' fair, Mr. Dancer."

"That boy has no kids to play with, and he misses his pa. I got a half eagle here. Five dollars in gold."

Smithers wrinkled his nose. "Not enough."

"I got two of them. Ten dollars."

"For the runt?"

"Yes," Colby said, playing with the bigger pup but reaching now for the smaller one, touching its wet nose and then picking it up in his arms. He stood up, playing with it, and the puppy chewed on his hand.

"All right," Smithers said, "but my wife will kill me."

"With ten dollars, she could buy some new dresses."

"Don't be givin' her ideas."

Colby gave him the two gold pieces, and he and Kansas left in mid afternoon. They were not sorry to leave the smell of the hog pen, and the pup bounced around in Colby's arms. It was

93

a good feeling, the soft furry bundle filled with fun and joy, chewing on Colby's hand.

As they rode, Kansas glanced over at him. "I was a runt, and I turned out all right."

"That's your opinion."

"You keep playing with that pup, you won't want to give it away."

Colby cradled it in his left arm as small teeth chewed on the sleeve of his shirt. "I had a dog when I was six. It died on me. Never got another."

"That's your problem, son. You got a glass wall built around you. Never let anyone get too close to you. Now I figure your sister was the exception."

"Are you Kansas now? Or the preacher?"

"The preacher."

"I like Kansas better. He keeps his mouth shut."

Kansas grinned and didn't answer.

As they followed the wagon road west once more, Kansas admired the distant cattle and horses. "Purvis would sure like to get his hands on this."

At the corrals of the Ramsey ranch, Hobbs greeted them as they dismounted to loosen the cinches and water their mounts. The old cowhand held the pup, playing with it.

"Mrs. Ramsey home?" Colby asked.

"Out with the herd."

"Jones boys come back?"

"Nope."

"And Tommy?"

"Up at the house, doing his letters. Is the pup for him?"

"Sure is."

Hobbs grinned broadly, showing a missing tooth. "Mr. Dancer, that's going to be one happy young fellow. Come on, I'll walk up with you. Got to see his face."

In the front room, seated at a table, Tommy was fighting with a pencil and looked sleepy, his left arm still in the sling. Hobbs sat down opposite him, and the boy made a face.

"I hate this stuff."

"You got company," Hobbs said.

Colby stood with his hat over the pup, still cradled in his arm, and Tommy smiled with delight at seeing him.

"This is my friend Kansas," Colby said. "And I got another friend, but he doesn't have a name. I figured you'd want to take care of that."

Tommy's eyes went round as Colby lifted his hat to reveal the pup, which was squirming to be set down.

"You mean, it's for me?" Tommy asked.

"If your ma says it's okay."

Tommy nearly fell out of the chair, and he stumbled forward, then rushed to reach out for the pup. When he grabbed it with his right hand, he lost his balance and went over backwards, landing on his rear with a plop, the pup still in his grasp.

The pup jumped up and scrambled about on top of his legs, barking at him, and Tommy laughed, trying to catch the little fur ball. He pulled his arm out of the sling, and now he and the pup were playing gleefully.

Later that afternoon, the three men sat on the porch, watching Tommy running around the grounds with his pup, but Hobbs was getting worried.

"Mrs. Ramsey should be back. It's going to be dark soon."

"We'd better have a look."

Tommy picked up his pup and came running back to the porch. "Want to know what I call him? Dancer."

Colby felt his face redden. This wonderful boy had named a pup after him. It was almost worth the pain that had brought Colby to this place.

It was near twilight when Colby and Kansas reached the herd, and Red was the only rider in sight.

"Mrs. Ramsey? She headed for Red Rock Canyon around noon, so she should have been home by now. Come on, I'll go with you."

CHAPTER TEN

Darkness crowding them as they crossed the rolling hills, the three men were worried. Red, because he admired Mrs. Ramsey. Kansas, because he didn't want any woman in danger. And Colby, because he realized he was emotionally attached to that woman, and it would be unbearable to find her dead or harmed.

"There's the entrance to Red Rock Canyon," Red told them. "She ain't never stayed out overnight before, but maybe her horse got lame or something."

They entered the canyon and rode along the stream in the moonlight. It was cold, icy.

"Look," Kansas said, pointing.

They looked up to the cliffs and the sheer walls of rock. There at the ledge high up near the rear of the canyon, where Colby had seen the streaks of gold some two hundred feet up from the canyon floor, they could see the figure of a woman.

She had fallen but had landed in brush just below the ledge and was hanging there precariously. She was either dead or afraid to move. Colby's heart stopped so long he couldn't breathe.

"My God," Red said.

"How did she get up there?" Kansas asked.

"I know how," Colby said. "But Red, you give me your rope and stay down below. Try to pile up some brush, anything in case she falls. Where she is, there's no way she's gonna land in the cottonwood like I did. Try to break her fall. Come on, Kansas."

Leaving Red to frantically wait below the dangling figure in the moonlight, Colby and Kansas rode out of the canyon and over to the foot of the steep climb. Here they found her horse in the pines. Taking their ropes, hers and Red's, they left their mounts and started up the steep grade, slipping and sliding.

"Wish that moon was brighter," Kansas said.

Colby prayed silently as they climbed.

When they reached the height of the deer trail, Colby could see she had been scraping the color off the sheer wall.

Heart pounding from more than the exercise, Colby moved along the ledge to where she had fallen. It was six feet wide in that area, backed by boulders.

On his knees, he leaned over and looked down at her upturned face. Her brown eyes were open wide and glistening, lips parted in terror. Her bloody hands gripped the brush that was barely holding her. Her right boot was hooked on a rock just below her while her other leg was dangling. Her holster was empty.

Colby lay on his stomach and leaned over, gripping her small wrist. His touch brought tears to her eyes, and she was close to hysteria.

"Now, Mrs. Ramsey," Colby said, "do you think if we lower a rope you could put it around you?"

She frantically shook her head, and her voice was hollow. "I can't let go."

"Then I've got to get a hold of you."

Colby was frantic. If he grabbed both of her wrists to pull her up, she could still slip from his grasp. He had to get a rope around her somehow. He lay holding her left wrist in his big right hand, waiting.

Kansas fastened the ropes around a boulder, and one loop went over Colby's waist. Another loop was in Colby's left hand, and he was lowering it past Melina's frightened face.

"Can you put your left foot in this loop?"

She was near hysterical, afraid to look down, but when the hondo bumped her leg, Melina slid her left boot into the loop, and Colby pulled it tight so that she could feel the security of it.

Colby had to fight his own fear of falling, remembering his horror, but there was no way he could leave her where she was. Any moment that brush could give way. He tried to look only at her and not the ghastly drop to the canyon floor.

Leaning down with another rope, he could feel the safety of the ledge leaving him. Only the ropes were holding him now, and he was terrified for both of them. Her small wrist seemed to be sliding in his grasp.

"Mrs. Ramsey," he said, "I'm going to put this rope around you, but I need both hands to do it. When it's tied, you have to let go."

She shook her head, her lips tight, eyes wild.

Quickly fastening the loop around her waist as he dangled next to her, he saw the brush slowly giving way from her bleeding hands, and now it tore from the cliff, dropping her as he grabbed her left wrist once more.

She screamed as she fell, but his grip and the ropes held her, and she bounced in mid-air. Terrified, she grabbed at Colby, seizing his shirt and arm, and he held tight to both of her wrists. She tried to grip his wrists with her small fingers.

"It's all right," he said. "Now listen to me. We're going to pull you up very slowly."

Colby prayed silently, worried the ledge itself could give way under the weight, and they could all go down. She closed her eyes tight and Kansas began to pull on the ropes. Still clutching her wrists, Colby drew her up slowly, but he was afraid he was going to go over himself and prayed his own rope would hold.

And now she was onto the ledge, grabbing at stone and moving over the rim, crawling to safety like a frightened child. Kansas pulled her against the boulders, then came to help Colby right himself.

As Colby sat down to rest, his chest heaving and heart thumping, he felt her bloody fingers grasp his gloved hand. Her lustrous hair and glorious eyes were shining in the moonlight. She was still badly shaken and looked like she might scream.

"Thank God," Kansas said.

Colby closed his eyes for a moment of silent prayer, giving thanks. They had both been so close to death, the thought was near unbearable.

Kansas freed and folded the ropes, and they put Melina between them. She clung to Colby's belt as he led the way back to safety in the pines. Once they were in the clear, she began to sob, but Colby pulled her wrists into his big hands while Kansas wrapped her palms and fingers with bandannas.

"You're okay," Kansas kept telling her.

They wouldn't let her rest, moving her between them down through the trees, stumbling in the moonlight, scratched by limbs, rocks rolling beneath their boots. The smell of cedar was strong in the night, and Colby was glad for it.

When they reached the horses, Kansas tightened the cinch on Melina's, and Colby took her by the waist, shaking her from her tears as he swung her up into the saddle, but she caught his hand before he could draw away.

"Colby?"

He swallowed hard at the sound of his name, for he was no longer Mr. Dancer to her, and he felt her hand squeezing his. He stared up at her wet face, his heart thumping.

"Come on," Kansas said. "We got to get out of here while there's still a moon. I see clouds moving in."

Red had seen the rescue and had a fire going by the rocky wall in the canyon, just under an outcropping of boulders because he expected rain. After washing her hands and putting bear grease on them, they bundled her up in blankets, for all three men had bedrolls and possibles. Only Red had a slicker, but they all had heavy coats.

Red made coffee and served beans. The night was frigid and damp, the cold reaching their bones.

By the time they had finished eating, the sky was dark and ominous. The crackling fire was the only light and warmth in the surrounding chill of the night.

"It's going to rain right soon," Red told them.

Colby turned to Melina. "What were you doing up there?"

She shrugged, glancing at Kansas. "I was just looking, and I tripped on a loose rock and fell over backwards. Did you see Tommy? Is he all right?"

"Yeah, I brought him a present. I hope you let him keep it. A pup I got from Smithers."

She brightened. "Oh, thank you, Colby. I'm so glad. He's been getting very difficult as of late. He needs friends his age, I know, and there are none in the valley."

Kansas poured her another cup of coffee. "That's a fine boy you have. When's his father coming back?"

"Soon," she said, glancing at Colby.

As they bundled into their own blankets, the men kept an eye on Melina.

And while they were huddled around the fire in the canyon, Jackson was in town, watching a stranger with wild blue eyes, a scar on the bridge of his large nose, and a black beard neatly trimmed, as he put up his horse in the lamplight of the livery barn. The man was wearing a black coat and hat, conchos on his hat band, and a silver trimmed gunbelt with twin holsters. His Colts had pearl handles.

"Mighty fine bay you have there."

"Cost me enough. Is Purvis in town?"

"Yeah, sure, across the bridge at the saloon."

The stranger left the barn and headed south, crossing the bridge in the starlight. He noted the bright lights of the gambling hall to his right and saw the crowd inside, and he knew the lights in the hotel meant a lot of activity.

But Miles Keo never got excited about much of anything. When he entered the Silver Dollar, he enjoyed the anxiety displayed by Purvis, who took him hurriedly to his office.

"About time you got here, Miles. But where's Mickey?"

"A day or so behind. He was busy with some female when I left Pine Ridge, and I got tired of waiting."

"As soon as he gets here, I have a job for you. I'm going after the finest ranch in this part of Montana. Ramsey's place, the Rockin' R."

Miles set his hat straight. "And where is Ramsey?"

"I got proof he's dead. Skip and Max are working for the widow. I guess you heard about Billy being killed. Now there's only six hands out there, but none of them fancy with a gun."

"Should be easy enough."

"Except for a couple of problems. One of them is Colby Dancer. He's hanging around out there."

Miles frowned, working his mouth. "I heard of Colby Dancer, all right. Man hunter for the cattlemen down along the Powder River. I'm not worried about him. Who else?"

"Kansas Grange."

"I thought he was dead."

"He's making himself out to be a preacher. But I'm not sure you can handle Kansas. You may be out of practice."

Miles shook his head. "Four hours a day. Mickey and I both."

"Good. Now, Skip got a bullet in his left arm when he and Max tried to dry gulch Dancer."

"Those two were never very smart."

"You're right about that. But Skip'll be okay. He's over at the hotel resting up. By the time Mickey gets here, he'll be ready to move."

CHAPTER ELEVEN

Late morning the next day, it was drizzling rain when Melina, Colby and Kansas returned to the ranch, Red having gone back to the herd. A frantic Tommy came running out of the house and down to the corrals. As she dismounted, he fell into Melina's arms, hugging her as she knelt.

"I'm all right, Tommy. Colby and his friend, Kansas, and Red, they came to rescue me. I'd fallen off a ledge in Red Rock Canyon. But everything's all right now."

"That's a bad place," Tommy said. "Don't go there no more."

"I won't go alone," she said.

"Mom, Mr. Dancer got me a pup! I named him Dancer."

"That's wonderful, Tommy."

"He likes me, Mom."

She smiled, then turned to Kansas and Colby. "Please, come on up to the house when you're ready."

Kansas tipped his hat in the rain. "If it's all the same to you, ma'am, I'm going on into town to look around."

She walked back to touch his arm, then she stood on her

tiptoes and kissed his hairy cheek. "Thank you, Kansas."

With Tommy at her side, she headed for the house, and Kansas was stricken, his mouth twisted as he tried to accept her gentle kiss.

Kansas swung into the saddle and Colby walked over to him, his hand on the pommel. "Listen, Kansas, I know you're fancy with a gun, but if Miles and Mickey show up, you sit tight. I'll be along in a couple days."

"I'm not worried about either one."

"Just don't trust anybody."

"You worried about me, son?"

"I'm not your darned son."

Kansas grinned and turned his horse toward town. Colby watched him ride away as the rain grew heavier, and he pulled down his hat brim, then tugged at his coat collar. He hurried up to the house where he found Tommy on the porch as rain pounded on the roof. The boy was playing with his pup.

"Mom says I got to train Dancer so he goes outside."

Colby knelt to play with the pup's floppy ears. "He'll make a good cowdog someday."

"Mom says you and Kansas saved her life."

"We were lucky, that's all."

"Mom says God sent you both."

Colby swallowed, his lips dry. "You'll get cold out here. Come on inside."

"No, I got to wait until Dancer goes."

Inside the house, Colby found Hobbs sitting by the fire and no sign of Melina. Colby pulled off his coat, hooked it on the wall, and shook the wet from his hat. Then he drew a chair up by the hearth to warm his cold hands.

"I'm gettin' too old for these winters up here," Hobbs said. "I'm going to be eighty-four right soon. My bones know every time the weather changes. Maybe I ought to head down to Arizona. Got friends in Tucson."

"Where's Mrs. Ramsey?"

"Right here," she said, entering with three cups of steaming coffee. She had changed her clothes and was wearing a heavy, blue wrapper, tucked in at the collar. She handed them each a cup, then sat down close to the crackling flames with the other cup in both hands.

"Mrs. Ramsey told me what happened to her," Hobbs said. "That canyon is jinxed."

"Why did Kansas ride off?" she asked Colby.

"He's a restless man."

Melina's face went pale, and she tightened her hold on her cup. "I've been thinking. What if Max and Skip showed my letter to Purvis? Maybe that's why Purvis was so brazen. Colby, I'm afraid."

"I think you can trust Hobbs here."

She nodded and took time to explain it to Hobbs, who was amazed at her story of Ramsey's death, his eyes round.

"Mrs. Ramsey, I wish you'd have asked for my help. But now I know for sure that canyon is jinxed. Colby here rolls off the cliff, and then you fall off a ledge. And now you tell me Mr. Ramsey was killed in a fall out there."

Melina hugged herself. "I'm afraid Purvis is going to ride on the ranch. All he needs is the right opening. Maybe tomorrow. Maybe next month. I don't know, but the way he acted, he's going to make a move."

Colby savored his coffee. "How loyal are the men here?"

"Red and Mitts, they're fine," Hobbs said. "The other three, they're old timers, spent most of their lives on the cattle trail. I suspect they wouldn't run from a fight. They'd ride for the brand all the way."

"We can't hold them off here," Colby said.

Melina put a hand to her throat. "I can't let them take Tommy's inheritance right out from under him."

"You and Tommy could go to Smithers's place."

"We can send Tommy, but we can't tell him why, and he'll go because he has fun with the chickens and pigs, and the Smithers dote on him. But I'm staying."

Hobbs shook his head. "No law out here. The folks on the north side of the creek are too scared to help. All Purvis has to do is lay siege until we give up."

"I figure we got some time," Colby said. "Now down by the creek and up at Red Rock Canyon, there's plenty of rock. And the ground will be soft from the rain. I figure we'll dig some trenches around the house and fortify them with rocks."

Melina was still shaken, and she left the room.

Hobbs turned to Colby. "She may be worried for nothing."

"We've both been around a long time, Hobbs. What do you think Purvis will do if he knows Ramsey is dead?"

"He'll ride on the ranch."

By Friday afternoon, the trenches were dug and wagon loads of rocks had been laid around them. The rain had let up long enough for the job to be done. Now the storm was breaking up for good, and Colby was pacing in front of the fire while Melina and Hobbs watched him from their chairs. Tommy was upstairs, playing with his pup.

"I'm going to town," Colby said, coming to a halt. "But you

keep Max and Skip busy out here, if they ever show up, that is."

Melina looked frightened. "No, Colby. You're not in the right frame of mind. You'll take chances."

"I've been thinking how Friday night is real quiet in town. Saturday, it'll be crowded. Too many in the way."

"Colby, I'll go with you," Hobbs said. "You need someone to watch your back."

But Colby insisted that Hobbs stay on the ranch to watch out for Melina and the boy. Minutes later, Colby headed for the door, coat and slicker in hand, bedroll and saddlebags under his arm. He just had to get going.

Out on the porch, Colby turned to see Melina closing the door behind her. The wind was rising, and the rain was blowing at them sideways, tossing her hair about her face.

She drew her shawl tightly about her and moved closer. "Colby, it's too dangerous in town. If Purvis really is making plans, they'll try to pick you off."

"I got no choice."

"If I wasn't so stubborn about the ranch—"

Tears filled her eyes, and he dropped his slicker as he reached out to place his hand on her small shoulder, feeling the softness, the tingling of her blowing hair.

"You're the bravest woman I ever knew."

She started to move toward him, but he held her at arm's length, his heart pounding up to his throat. If he was to take her in his arms right now, he'd be a goner.

"Colby, I owe you so much. Tell me what to do."

"If I'm not back on Sunday, send the boy to Smithers's place. Hobbs can tell Tommy it's to play with both pups so they don't get lonesome. And Hobbs can tell Smithers the truth."

He released her shoulder, picked up his slicker, and turned to the edge of the porch, forcing himself toward the rain as he started to pull on his coat.

"Colby."

He paused, unable to move, and she was behind him, her arms around his waist, her face pressed hard to his back. Heart wild, breathless, he stood with the rain blowing on his face, his hands at his side, unable to move.

But now she was turning him, forcing him to look down at her hot face and shining, wet eyes. Streaks of sunlight streaming through the downpour struck her hair like satin.

"Colby, please come back."

He swallowed so hard it hurt, and then he held his breath as she moved against his chest, sliding her arms around him and gazing up at him as if he was some kind of hero, and that was mighty hard to take.

She stood on her tiptoes, lips parted, gazing up at him beseechingly. Grim, he tried to stop his arms from sliding around her, but there they went as his coat and everything else fell to the porch floor. He didn't want to crush her, but he was already holding her so tight he was afraid he would hurt her.

And then he bent his head so that his lips met hers.

The kiss sent chills racing through him like bolts of lightning, and he kept kissing her lips, then her cheeks and small nose, tasting the woman of her.

With superhuman effort, he broke free and stepped back, holding his breath until he could spin around and pick up his coat, which he hurriedly pulled on again with shaking hands. Then he picked up his gear. He headed into the hesitant rain.

"Come back, Colby."

Her plaintive voice drove him onward. The clouds were breaking up and the sun was streaking through, leaving a rainbow at the east end of the valley.

When he was near the Ramsey gate, he came on Mitts with the wagon loaded with supplies, on his way back from town. The cowhand reined, waving to him, and Colby rode over.

"Colby, I got bad news. It's Kansas. He was bushwhacked in the street last night. He's over at the barber's now. He took a bullet, but it didn't hit no vitals, went clean through, back of his left shoulder. He's just resting up at the barber's."

"Darn it."

"Nobody knows who done it, but I saw Skip and Max laughing it up this morning outside the gambling hall."

Colby pulled down his hat tight and started to ride past, but Mitts reached out a hand to slow him.

"There's something else, Colby. New face in town. They say it's Miles Keo."

Sweat on his face and neck, ice-blue eyes shadowed by angry brows, Colby turned his sorrel. "What does he look like?"

"Wearing a black coat. Got conchos on his hat band. Scar on his nose. Big nose. Silver on his gunbelt. Got a short beard trimmed around his jaw. No mustache. Looks mean as heck."

CHAPTER TWELVE

Friday nights were tamer than Saturdays, but Colby still sensed the danger as he dismounted in front of the Silver Dollar. His six-guns were oiled and loaded. Tense, he removed his coat and tied it over his bedroll. Then he pushed his Stetson back from his damp brow. His fingers were tight, and he shook them, letting them dangle at his sides.

He wanted to see Kansas, but this couldn't wait.

It was pretty certain Miles Keo had been at the robbery in Slye. He was the man with the scar on his nose, something the bandanna had not covered, a vicious man.

Hate had been churning in Colby for two years.

Peering in the window of the Silver Dollar, he could see Purvis behind the bar, counting his money as usual. The bartender was busy with two hardcases at the left end of the bar, their backs turned, and one wearing a black coat, conchos on his hat band.

At a table near the right wall were three rough looking men playing cards and drinking heavily. The redhead was plunked down in a chair near them, and she looked half asleep. He had never seen a less enthusiastic painted lady.

Across the street, the hotel had lights glowing in every room, and the gambling hall looked crowded. There was no sign of Skip and Max.

Colby swallowed hard and made sure his six-guns were loose in their holsters. He moved to enter through the bat-wing doors, and as he walked slowly forward, he noticed that the three men at the table pretended not to see him.

Purvis looked up with a grimace, while the bartender merely stared. The two men at the end of the bar turned very slowly. The one in the black coat had wild blue eyes. The other was sloppy drunk and scratching a heavy beard as he leaned over the bar.

"Dancer," Purvis said.

The man in the black coat straightened and made a full turn to look Colby over. His voice was cold and sharp.

"So you're Colby Dancer."

Colby moved past the table where the men were playing cards, and he stood at the end of the bar with his back to the wall. He was three feet from Purvis and a dozen feet from the man in the black coat. Sweat was running down his back and rear, but he spoke quietly.

"Are you Miles Keo?"

"That's right."

"Drink on the house, Dancer?" Purvis asked. "It could be your last."

Colby stood with feet apart, gazing past Purvis to Miles Keo. "No, thanks. I don't drink Keos whiskey."

Purvis stiffened. "Now, Mr. Dancer, you've been listening to that crazy Kansas Grange."

"Where are Skip and Max?"

"You just missed them."

"And Mickey Keo?"

"Why, he's not here," Purvis said.

Colby glared at Miles Keo. "You and Mickey were in Slye two years ago, robbing the bank."

The heavily bearded drunk quickly left the bar and plunked down at a corner table. Miles Keo straightened very slowly, a snicker passing his lips.

"You could be right, Dancer. What are you going to do about it?"

"Make a citizen's arrest of an escaped convict."

"You'd have to arrest the whole town."

"You're the one I want."

"I have no fight with you."

Colby moistened his lips. "You got one, whether you want it or not."

From the corner of his eye, Colby could see that the redhead was crossing the room to where the drunk had collapsed. The three men at the table, off to his left, had grown mighty quiet.

Colby spoke calmly, his mouth dry. "A woman was killed at that robbery in Slye. They say your brother Mickey pulled the trigger, but you were there."

Miles Keo slid his left hand across the bar a few inches and studied Colby. "That so?"

"The woman was my sister."

Miles' blue eyes went dark. "Sorry to hear that."

Colby was drenched with sweat now and yet his skin was frozen, chilled, stiffening. He wondered if his fingers would move fast enough. He was a fool to have come alone.

Hands at his sides, Colby waited for Miles to react to his stance. Purvis and the bartender hurriedly backed away to the office entrance on Colby's right.

Miles Keo smiled, his dangerous eyes gleaming. "Maybe you can take me, maybe you can't. Go ahead and try, Dancer."

"You're under arrest, Keo."

Miles forced a short laugh. "Dancer, you're a dead man."

They moved a few steps from the bar, and Colby, a bare wall behind him, was still aware of the men at the table, knowing they could take a hand against him. Yet the dice had already been rolled, and here he was, facing one of the men who had caused his sister's death.

"All right, Colby, make your play."

Miles frowned, brows lowering to nearly hide his eyes, and his mouth was working at the corner. Any minute now…

Suddenly, Miles drew fast and sure.

But Colby drew at the same time, and both men fired.

Colby's bullet slammed into Miles' chest, dead center.

Miles' bullet grazed the left side of Colby's head, spinning him around. He crashed against the wall and dropped to one knee, dazed and not seeing clearly but raising his sixgun.

Abruptly, a bullet went sideways into his back above his left shoulder, leaving a painful crease, and he dropped to both knees, shock racing through him. He turned to see the man at the table lifting his sixgun. Colby fired, hitting him in the middle of his gut, and the man squealed, falling backward.

Near unconscious from the bullet's blow to his head, Colby saw the other two men jump up and start firing. He was vaguely aware of more gunfire as he fell face down on the floor, unconscious.

In the doorway, Jackson was holding two six-guns. He had downed the men at the table, but had taken a bullet in his left arm just below the shoulder.

Only the drunk, the frightened woman, the barkeep, and Purvis were unhurt. Miles Keo lay dead and flat on his back with his mouth open. Jackson moved slowly forward, keeping his back to the side wall as he barked at them.

"You there, both of you behind the bar. Pick him up, and I mean now."

Nervous, the bartender followed Purvis around the bar, stepping over the dead Miles Keo. They struggled to pick up the dazed Colby, who was a big man and holding tight to his six-guns.

"Take him outside to his horse."

"He's bleeding," the bartender said.

"Just do as I say."

The two men ended up half dragging Colby across the floor and past the other dead men who were sprawled around the table in their chairs. Jackson had tied a bandanna around his arm to stop the bleeding.

It was cold and dark with only the outside lamp to guide them to the sorrel. They set Colby in the saddle, his mount snorting and jumping as Jackson holstered his six-guns, then Jackson growled at the two men.

"Get back inside, and I don't want to see any faces at the window."

Purvis looked grim as he and the barkeep backed inside the saloon. Jackson stuck one sixgun in his belt, keeping the other trained on the saloon as he picked up the reins of the sorrel, walking sideways toward the bridge.

No one at the hotel or gambling hall had even bothered to look outside, despite the many shots.

Jackson crossed the bridge then put the sorrel at a trot as he ran along side to keep Colby from falling.

The little, near-bald barber was half asleep and overwhelmed by Jackson's bleeding and Colby's head wound. Realizing he was safe and seeing Kansas peacefully asleep on the couch, Colby passed out as they put him on a table. Colby lay lifeless while the barber tried to clean the wounds.

"Can't do nothin' for that head wound," the barber said. "A lot of 'em like that in the War. Some never came out of it. His back's okay. Just a crease."

The barber turned his attention on Jackson, who was slumped in a chair, exhausted.

Later, Miles Keo was dumped on the boardwalk outside, but Jackson wouldn't let the barber even look at Miles until dark. Kansas awakened to hear the story, and he was able to sit up, despite his heavy bandages. Hours passed into the night, and still Colby lay unconscious.

"He ain't going to make it," the barber said.

Jackson waved the sixgun at him. "He'd better, or I'll part what hair you got left."

CHAPTER THIRTEEN

Purvis couldn't believe that Miles Keo was dead, and when he dropped down in a chair in his office, dignity somewhat shaken, the incredulous Max and Skip came charging into the room, slamming the door behind them. They pulled up chairs with a squeak on his polished floor.

Max shook his head in disbelief. "Darn. Just wait till Mickey gets here. He'll tear this town apart."

"Did Dancer really beat Miles to the draw?" Skip asked.

"Clean as a whistle," Purvis said. "Bullets were flying right after. If Jackson hadn't come along, I would have finished Dancer myself. I always hated that black devil. If this was Georgia, we'd have hanged him by now."

"Let's do it anyway," Skip said.

Purvis shook his head. "He's the only smithy in town."

"Things ain't so bad," Max said. "Skip got Kansas in the back, and Dancer's down, maybe for good. Jackson got hit in the arm. All three are out of it. Maybe we don't have to wait for Mickey to ride on the Ramsey place."

Skip agreed. "All they got out there now is a bunch of cowhands. Hobbs, he's too darn old. Mitts can't hit the side of a barn. Red, he's real nervous. The other three, they got no reason to fight."

Purvis studied them with contempt. They were his nephews, but Purvis was the thinker, not them. He straightened his collar and stood up slowly.

"You boys get some rest. Come morning, there'll be some sorry gamblers with empty pockets, looking for easy money."

"Heck," said Max, "we won't need many of them."

"We don't want a bloody fight," Purvis said. "The more of us, the easier it will be. And remember, I don't want a hand laid on Melina Ramsey."

"What about the boy?" Max asked.

"I don't care about him. He's Ramsey's whelp, not mine."

"So when are we going?"

"Sunday morning, afore sunup."

"Why wait?" Max asked. "I'm ready now."

"You boys never stop to think. Now, some of Ramsey's men could be in town on Saturday. We don't want them to pick up any warnings, and we don't want any trouble in town. Besides, we need the element of surprise. Now get out of here. I have some plans to make."

Max made a face. "We wait too long, Kansas and Dancer could get better."

"Not a chance," Purvis said. "Skip got Kansas in the back. And Dancer, he's still unconscious. Jackson'll be shaking in his boots about now, scared of us, and for good reason."

Skip wrapped his arms about himself. "Uh, Purvis, we was over at the gambling hall, and those tables of yours are right crooked, and we could sure use some money."

"That all you ever think about? Women and whiskey and gambling?" Purvis asked.

But they talked him out of some money, and they took off through the saloon, headed for the gambling hall. Purvis returned to his desk with a smile, for he knew he had them both under his control.

On Saturday afternoon, Seth Dancer reined up at the general store. Wearing a fringed leather coat, he was a big man in his late twenties with sandy hair and light blue eyes. He had a day's growth of beard, a hard jaw and wide thin lips, and he moved easily as he dismounted. He looked around the town, then walked into the cluttered store, pushing back his tattered Stetson.

The storekeeper in his white apron, pale face clean shaven, receding hairline and pot belly, was friendly enough, but suspicious, for he figured the stranger was just another gunslinger.

"Need some ammunition," Seth said. "And some information."

"This ain't no newspaper."

"I heard a lot about this town. South side full of outlaws. North side, hiding like rats."

The storekeeper frowned. "You're wearin' out your welcome, mister. What do you want?"

Seth paid for the bullets and looked around the store, then checked out a new black Stetson, tried it on and bought it also, tossing his old one aside.

"Well, sir, I'm looking for Colby Dancer."

"What for?"

"I'm his brother Seth."

"Well, why didn't you say so? He's been shot. Over at the barber's, next building up the street. Him and that friend of his, Kansas Grange. And the smithy, too. All three shot up. Dancer killed Miles Keo last night, and he already killed two more afore that. Word is Colby Dancer is the fastest gun in the West."

"Maybe he is, maybe not."

Seth grabbed his purchases and rushed outside onto the boardwalk, startling his bay as he hurried past. Sweat formed on his face and neck, and his boots clumped on the boardwalk in a fast rush to the next building.

The barber let him in with surprise. "Didn't know he was expecting a brother."

"He's not. Where is he?"

"Back room."

Seth pushed past him to the back room where Kansas was sitting up, his left arm in a sling and color back in his face. Jackson was propped up in a chair with his left leg on a stool, his left arm bandaged and in a sling as well.

On the table, Colby lay unconscious. A frantic Seth hurried to his side and touched Colby's face, then paced back and forth as he introduced himself. Kansas was staring at him in dismay while Jackson told the whole story of what he had been missing.

"So now what?" Seth asked.

"Purvis figures we're all out of commission," Kansas said, "and he'll ride on the ranch as soon as he picks a few hardcases to back him up. I don't figure he'll wait for Mickey, not now. They could leave as early as Sunday morning. Tomorrow."

"I can ride," Jackson said. "I'll head on out and warn Mrs. Ramsey. They didn't get my gun arm."

"I can ride, too," Kansas said. "I've been shot up a lot worse than this and never left the saddle. Hurts like heck, but it ain't stopping me."

Jackson was worried. "Somebody's got to stay here and keep Purvis from finishing Colby off."

"Nobody's touching my brother."

They looked at Seth's size and his well-oiled Colts, and Kansas grinned. "You Dancers come big."

"There's three more of us down in Socorro."

"We'll go after dark," Jackson said. "If Colby's awake by then, maybe we can take him with us. Head wounds can heal up real fast, once he wakes up."

But they were all thinking the same thing, that maybe Colby would never open his eyes again.

Colby was still unconscious when Saturday night came, and the patched-up Kansas and Jackson slipped out of town, heading west on the north side of the creek, planning to ford it later when they were out of sight of town.

Seth stayed to watch over his brother and had supper brought in to him. Once, he went outside to gaze toward the bridge, but he didn't see anything in particular, just a lot of men moving about. He wasn't ready to let them know there was another Dancer in town. He wanted surprise on his side.

The barber came from time to time and would shake his head, recounting how soldiers with head wounds had sometimes never awakened, or if they did, had brain damage. Seth became angry and sent him out of the back room for good.

Late afternoon on Sunday, Seth was dozing on the couch when he heard a sound. He sat up, Colt in hand, about to jump up when he saw Colby sitting upright.

Seth holstered his sixgun with a big grin, leaped to his feet and rushed over to the table to grab Colby's arm. "Thank God."

"Where did you come from?" Colby asked, his head spinning as he blinked, trying to clear his vision. He winced because his back still hurt from the bullet's crease, and he had one bad headache.

Seth hugged him carefully. "I got your letter and hopped every train and coach I could find to get up here. And I already heard what's been goin' on, and how you got Miles."

"Mickey's on his way here."

"We'll get 'im, but Kansas and Jackson went out to the Rockin' R to try to hold off Purvis Keo and his bunch. Kansas looks all right now, moving around pretty good, and Jackson was only hit in the arm. Seems like Jackson saved your life."

"That's the second time," Colby said. "He don't like the idea much."

"He's a good man. But how'd you ever meet up with Kansas Grange? I hear he's a real bad one. Killed maybe twenty men in his time, most in gunfights."

"He was pretending to be a preacher, and then he kind of attached himself to me. Says he wants the men who raided Slye, himself, but he ain't said why. He acts a little strange sometimes. But then so does everybody else around here."

"Storekeeper says killin' Miles Keo makes you the fastest gun in the West, but I figure I can still out-draw you anytime."

Colby grinned, shook his head and winced at the dizziness. "Where's Purvis now?"

"I don't know. It's real quiet south of the bridge."

"We got to get moving. There's a woman and a boy. They could get hurt."

"Kansas said you were makin' eyes at her."

Colby's face turned hot. "Kansas talks too much."

"Well, when I got your letter about how you were comin' to Dead Man's Creek and the Ramsey ranch, I did some checkin' right off. Lou Ramsey ran with the Keos for a time. He could have been at Slye."

"Ramsey's dead." Colby filled him in on the hidden grave and managed to stand a bit shakily. "Hobbs and the boy are the only ones who know she buried Ramsey."

"Sounds like quite a woman. Maybe I ought to meet her myself."

Colby straightened, glaring at him. "Forget it."

Seth grinned. "So you ain't dead yet."

"We can both forget about her. I figure once this trouble is over, she could do a lot better than me or you. But right now, we'd better get on out there. As soon as I get something to eat."

"Sure you can ride?"

"Yeah, I can see all right now." And Colby slowly unwound the bandage from his head.

While the brothers helped themselves to a quick meal at the Red Feather, the Ramsey ranch was preparing for a lot of trouble.

That morning, Melina had sent Tommy to Smithers's place on the pretext of playing with the pups and visiting the elderly couple, and while there, Tommy was having a great time as usual. But in the afternoon on Sunday, he overheard the Smithers couple talking about the danger at the Rockin' R.

"I know Purvis is going after the ranch," Smithers said. "He's a greedy man, and I wager he won't care who gets in his way. I just hope Mrs. Ramsey don't get hurt. Ranch ain't worth much if you're dead. Although she's trying real hard to keep it together for the boy."

Listening from his room, Tommy became frantic and worried about his mother and the others. He pulled on his coat, left his pup playing with its brother, and slipped out the back window of the house with his small rifle. He ran to the corral and saddled his pinto pony.

Smithers came running outside as Tommy swung into the saddle. "Boy, wait! Your ma's going to have my hide."

"It ain't your fault."

"But you could get hurt."

"Mr. Smithers, I can hunt rabbit and squirrel, and I can ride and rope as good as anybody. I'm going to be ten years old next week, for gosh sakes."

Smithers stood shaking his head in disbelief.

Tommy turned his pony and headed across the meadows toward the wagon road and Ramsey gate. He hadn't gone far when he saw a dozen men near the creek, coming from town and heading for the gate. They were so far away, they looked like ants, but he knew it meant trouble.

Quickly, he headed for the cover of the rolling hills, knowing they could get there first even though they were riding at a walk, yet Tommy was determined to do his best.

As he rode, he thought of his cold, distant father, buried on the mountain near Red Rock Canyon. He could see his mother's lovely face and smile. And there was Dancer, that mysterious big man who chased rustlers and seemed to like Tommy.

Everything now seemed critical. Save the ranch. Save his mother. Save Dancer.

When he had plenty of cover, he set his pony to a gallop, but in no time, the pinto was losing its footing and sliding, crashing down, and rolling over on top of Tommy.

* * * * *

Kansas and Jackson were getting the six cowhands organized at the ranch. It was windy, and clouds were moving in from the north. Dark, ominous clouds. Evening was coming on fast.

Red was nervous, but he wouldn't run. Mitts thought it was going to be great sport, holding off an attack. The three grizzled hands who were veterans of the trail and could handle themselves were not enthusiastic, but they were staying.

Hobbs tried to get Melina to go to Smithers's farm.

"This is my ranch," she said, "and it's going to be Tommy's. What's more, I can shoot as good as any of you. Besides, look at that storm coming. No one will bother us until it's over. They might wait until we think they're not coming so they can surprise us."

"Too bad Mr. Ramsey ain't here," Mitts said as he heaped more rocks along the trenches.

Hobbs and Melina looked at each other, and she went back in the house to hide her fear.

Kansas couldn't do much but sit on a rock and give orders, but Jackson had one good hand, and he was piling more rocks than the able-bodied men. The trenches were about ready, but the men were worried about the storm filling them with water, so Kansas had them dig ditches downhill to drain.

* * * * *

Coming along the wagon road, following the creek and some twenty miles away as yet, Purvis and his two nephews rode some distance ahead of the five misfits they had gathered.

"It's a mistake," Max said. "We get the ranch, them fellahs you hired will try to take it away from us. Look at 'em. Ever see a meaner bunch? Especially that old guy with the red beard and the half-breed with one eye."

"Don't worry," Purvis said, "I can handle them with money."

Skip made a face. "I agree with Max."

Purvis turned in the saddle to look back at the five hairy, beady-eyed men in heavy coats with dirty hats. He didn't want to admit he was just as worried, but there was no turning back now.

While Purvis and his men headed west along the creek, Seth and Colby Dancer were riding as fast as they could, having learned from the barber that Purvis was on his way to the ranch.

"Tracks in the mud," Colby said. "Have a look."

Seth leaned from the saddle, gazing down in the twilight's last glow. "Maybe eight of 'em. And a good eight hours or more ahead of us. They might be there by now, but if it rains, it's gonna slow 'em down."

"They don't know they're expected. They think Kansas and Jackson are laid up, so they're gonna be plenty surprised. But the fight could go either way."

"I hope we're not too late."

CHAPTER FOURTEEN

Back at the house, Melina was serving an early supper to Kansas, who was fading and weak from his injuries. Jackson and Hobbs were outside, walking around in the darkness. Down in the trenches, the hands were pulling on their slickers.

Kansas fought to keep himself together, but he had been too quick to ignore the loss of blood. His hands were shaking, and Melina tried not to notice.

"Are you sure Mr. Dancer's going to be all right?"

"Ma'am, you couldn't kill him with an army. He's made of iron."

"Yes, he is."

Kansas smiled at her. "Like him, do you?"

"No, not at all. Mr. Dancer is made out of stone. I don't think he has any real feelings."

"Now, ma'am, there's something you don't know. When Colby was about nine, same as Tommy's is now, he and his father were hunting in the Colorado Rockies. Being the oldest of five boys, Colby was trying to be a man like his father. Well, the story is that his father was knocked out of the saddle by an arrow from some stray Ute or Cheyenne, and he fell down in a deep canyon."

Melina held her cup in both hands, listening in silence.

"Seems like Colby jumped off his horse and slid all the way down after him. The Indian, he took the horses and disappeared. The boy spent two days with his father dying in his arms, and he couldn't do anything about it. He had to bury him, and it took him two weeks to walk out of the mountains, all by himself."

Melina's eyes brimmed, and she stared into her coffee as he continued.

"He had four little brothers at home. One of 'em, Seth, had just been born. And a baby sister. Colby had to get home and tell his ma she was a widow. He was never the same after that. He became a man when he was still just a boy. He never learned how to have fun."

"How do you know all this?"

Kansas shrugged. "I had a letter once from his mother."

"You knew her?"

"It's a long story. Now why don't you get some rest? It's starting to rain, and tomorrow could be a real busy day. Keep your Winchester handy."

"What about you, Kansas? You look so pale."

"I'll sleep here by the fire. You don't worry about me."

*   *   *   *   *

Along the north side of the creek a half mile away in the moonlight, which came and went behind the clouds, Purvis had stopped his horse and was peering through the cottonwoods toward the house with a spyglass. They had purposely taken their time so they would arrive after dark.

"Looks like some kind of barrier, but they don't have enough men to circle the house all the time."

Skip frowned. "What can we do?"

"You and Max ride on ahead and cross the creek on the other side of the house. Sneak in there and get Mrs. Ramsey. Bring her out to me. And don't hurt her."

"It's startin' to rain," Max said, reaching for his slicker as the moon disappeared and the sky blackened with crackling noise. "They'll have to take cover. They could be in the house."

"But not upstairs where she sleeps. She's a respectable woman, so she'll be alone. You get in a back window."

"What if the kid's there?"

"Knock him on the head."

"I don't like it."

"The rain will be noisy. Lightning already. Just get in and out fast."

Up at the house, as the rain began to fill the trenches, the men fell back to the porch for shelter. Hobbs, his aching bones feeling the chill, went inside to warm himself by the hearth while Kansas slept. Soon Hobbs was dozing in a chair.

Jackson stayed on the porch with the men, but he had them take turns circling the house on patrol every so often. He warned them about the trees and lightning.

The rain became so heavy and dark, the grizzled cowhand on guard was walking behind the house when he slipped and fell in the mud, crashing up against an aspen and cussing.

Using the butt of his Winchester to right himself, the guard continued on around the house as lightning flashed on the horizon and the rain pounded him.

Max and Skip, huddled in the trees, stood up and moved to the back of the house. There was a back door, but it was locked. Along side the house, there was a tall aspen with branches only two feet from a window, and Max reined up close to it.

"You take the horses back down behind the trees," Max said. "When you see me coming out the back door with her, you come fast. But if you see someone coming, make like an owl."

"What owl's gonna be hootin' in this rain?"

"All right, don't do nothin'. Just wait till it's clear."

Max got up in the saddle, standing on it, as Skip held his horse's head, and soon Max was up in the thick branches and leaning over to the dark window as Skip took the horses away.

Max waited until he saw another guard pass, and when there was no one in sight, he easily forced the window with his hunting knife and climbed inside.

It was an empty room with the door open. Light from the hallway lamp told him it was a boy's room, but he saw no sign of Tommy. There were three other rooms. The first two were not occupied. That meant if Melina was in the house, she was in the room at the end of the hall.

Max was conscious of his squeaking boots and dripping slicker, but there was no time to waste. He slowly opened the door as the lamplight filtered past him.

Melina was asleep in her clothes and boots on top of the bed, lustrous hair across her pillow. Her Winchester leaned against the bedpost, and her heavy coat was on a chair.

He wet his lips, and an urge made him burn with lust. Yet

there wasn't time, and he picked up a folded blanket from the top of the dresser, spreading it open.

As he neared the bed, she stirred.

Her eyes opened just as he shoved the blanket down on her face to muffle her scream. She fought furiously, and he slammed his fist into her jaw. She collapsed in his hands, unconscious. Max grabbed her heavy coat off the chair.

Lifting her to a sitting position, he pulled her coat around her as he fought his desperate need for her. Then he lifted her up and threw her over his shoulder. He carried her into the hallway and stopped to listen, but there was no sound from downstairs.

Carrying the lifeless woman slowly down the steps, he peered around the corner to see two men sleeping by the hearth. Holding his breath, he hurried to the back door, opened it from the inside, and peered out into the dark rain, waiting. Now he saw the guard walking some ten feet away, and he swallowed hard, waiting until the man went around the house.

Almost immediately, Skip came riding out of the trees, leading Max's horse. Once Max got in the saddle with Melina thrown across in front of him, they headed back for the creek.

* * * * *

After midnight, Colby and his brother rode up to the corrals. Everything looked normal, and in a flash of lightning, they could see the men on the porch.

"They'd better stay out of those trees," Seth remarked. "The way that lightning's flashing, it's pretty dangerous."

They put their horses away, threw their gear in the tack room, and headed up the slope past the empty trenches and over to the porch to join the men. Colby introduced them to Seth, then surveyed the darkness around them.

"Nothing's happening," Red told him.

"Where's Mrs. Ramsey?"

"Asleep, I think. Tommy's over at Smithers's place."

Inside the house, the brothers found Kansas and Hobbs asleep in front of the hearth. After shedding their slickers and building up the fire, they heated up some coffee on the iron stove and settled down near the fire in the leather chairs, exhausted, and soon, they were asleep as well.

Around two in the morning, Colby awakened. The rain and wind were striking the house hard, and he felt the walls shudder. He rubbed his eyes and sat up straight. He knew that Melina was usually down by this time, starting a fire in the stove and readying breakfast.

He stood up and walked into the room with the stairway to the second floor. The back door was rattling, and he went over to close it tight. He noticed rain puddles around it. The wood floor was still wet all the way to the staircase.

He turned and ran up the stairs, taking three steps at a time. In the hallway, he paused, remembering his and Tommy's rooms, and he figured she had to be at the far end. Right hand on a Colt, he moved slowly forward.

When he found her room empty and the bedding in disarray, he felt horror that left him cold. He turned and sped back down the hallway and down the stairs, only slowing down when he saw Seth sitting up and yawning.

He beckoned to him and whispered that Melina was gone.

"You stay here. This is a one man job."

"Now hold on, Colby. I'm the only one ain't wounded."

"Listen to me, Seth. I figure they're across the creek. Can't be more than a few feet deep. I'll cross over and sneak up on 'em and get her back."

"I'm coming with you, darn it."

They awakened Kansas and Hobbs to tell them what was happening. Hobbs was furious, and Kansas, still in need of rest, could only wish them luck.

But across the creek, Purvis was fed up with the rain. The unconscious Melina was wrapped in blankets and covered with a slicker. Their five vicious hired hands were curled up in their blankets under tarps, further down the creek. Only Skip and Max were awake and on guard.

"You near killed her," Purvis told Max. "Well, I'm taking her out of here. She's our ace in the hole. You boys take out the ranch house, and I'll be back when you have it secured."

"You're running this show. So it's better if I take her."

Purvis glared at him in the downpour. "Listen to me, Max, and I don't want to say it again. Stay away from her. You boys aren't fit to kiss her feet."

"And you are?"

"That's right. I'm the brains of this outfit. I ran the show in Slye. You boys tried it in Pocket and ended up blowing Billy to heck. So just shut your mouths, and keep an eye on the house and these hired guns. I'll take her some place safe."

"Where?" Max asked, his face hot with anger.

"I'll get to town afore daylight. When you finish taking the house and killing everybody—and I mean everybody—you come tell me. I'll be in my office."

"What's to stop us from taking the place for ourselves?"

"Because I got Melina Ramsey, and she owns it."

133

"I don't like it," Max said. "I went in and got her. She's mine, darn it."

"I'm in charge. Now, do as I say."

Purvis pulled his dripping hat down tight and turned toward where Melina lay. Max grimly pulled his hunting knife from his saddle.

Before Purvis could take another step, Max stabbed him in the back with great fury, right through the heart. Purvis didn't cry out, but he grabbed at air, staggered down to his knees, and fell flat on his face in the mud and swirling water.

Skip came over, wide-eyed, and they spoke in whispers. "Holy cow, Max."

"Come on, we're taking her with us."

"What about the ranch?"

"She's all we need. When I marry her, we can come back and live peaceable. We're gonna sneak back along the creek to town afore daylight, pack up good, and keep going. Once we get us to a preacher, we'll have us a real spread."

"Why would she marry you?"

"Because I'm going to tell her a pack of lies."

"Like what?"

"I'll think of something. Maybe I'll tell her Purvis has got her kid and is gonna kill 'im if she don't marry me."

The cousins saddled up and left with the unconscious Melina bound and gagged and settled in Max's arms. They took the horses belonging to the sleeping hardcases they'd hired so no one would follow.

When Seth and Colby forded the creek bareback, the water was rising and tearing at them, but they made it across. Leaving their horses in the cottonwoods, they slowly moved east along the creek, boots slipping and sliding in the mud and heavy rain.

When they reached the outlaw camp, they found Purvis lying face down with a knife in his back. Saddles and blankets lay under tarps, but there was no sign of anyone else.

Until the lead started to fly.

CHAPTER FIFTEEN

Seth and Colby dove for cover in the trees and brush, even as lightning flashed overhead and crackled off into the night. Bullets were flying around them, and they could see the flashes of gunfire.

"I count five," Colby said. "You keep them busy. I'm going to circle."

Seth knelt down in the rocks and fired at a flash, and they heard a man yell in horrible pain. Colby moved into the rocks, and he saw a man crawling along on his hands and knees toward him.

When the man saw him, he leaped to his feet, red beard dripping wet, sixgun firing, even as Colby dodged to one side and fired back, hitting him in the gut, knocking him about and down on the ground.

Another man came running toward Colby, firing rapidly, and Colby shot him in the chest, dead center, sending him spinning and crashing into the brush. That was three.

He heard Seth fire, and another man yell. Four.

Now he turned to see a wild man with a patch over his eye, charging him with a blazing sixgun. Colby shot him in the heart, and the man jerked, doubled up, and fell.

It was over so fast, Colby could hardly catch his breath. Seth called to him, and Colby went back.

"One's still alive."

A grizzled man lay on his back in the rain as they shielded his face with his hat. He gazed up with wild, beady eyes, cussing them furiously, but he was slipping away fast.

"Where's Mrs. Ramsey?" Colby asked, kneeling.

"The Jones boys—"

The man coughed, rolled his eyes, and died. Colby lowered the hat to rest on the man's face, and he got to his feet, heart pounding.

"We've got to catch up with 'em."

Back at the house, they found Jackson, Kansas, and Hobbs near the fire. Kansas had his color back, and he stood up when he heard about Melina. Both he and Jackson were ready to ride.

Hobbs was furious. "Darn them. If they harm her—"

"We'll catch 'em," Colby promised.

"I'll have your horses saddled," Hobbs said. "You want some of us to go with you?"

"No," Colby said. "You and your men had better make sure no one else tries to move in here."

"I'll help saddle up," Jackson said, hurrying after Hobbs, both pulling on their slickers and closing the door on the rain and wind.

Kansas beckoned to Colby and Seth to wait, and they came to stand near him as he pulled on his heavy coat and aging Stetson.

"Boys, did your ma ever tell you about her renegade kid

brother, the one was run off when he was fourteen on account of a gunfight and never came back?"

Colby stared at him. "You're him?"

"Your uncle, boys."

"Why didn't you tell us?"

"'Cause I didn't think you'd want to be kin to the likes of me. You said it yourself, Colby."

Colby swallowed hard. "It's different now."

"You may not be proud of me, but I can tell you this, I'm sure proud of you boys. And I'm right sorry I never knew your sister, but your ma sent me her portrait when she was a little girl, and I still carry it. So, nobody's gonna get away with it."

The two men had wet eyes as they shook his hand, and then all three went outside into the night, pulling on their slickers. Rain was thundering on the porch roof, and lightning flashed in the distance.

"Come on," Red said, running up to the porch. "That's Tommy's pinto pony at the corral."

They hurried down to the nervous pony, but there was no sign of the boy. Colby felt his heart tugged in all directions.

"Don't worry," Hobbs said. "We'll find him. At least he's got his old single-shot rifle. And he's been bucked off before."

But Colby was so worried, his stomach was in a knot. First Melina carried off, and now Tommy missing.

The four riders headed along the north side of the creek, Seth and Colby in the lead, Jackson and Kansas following. Breaks in the storm gave way to moonlight now and then.

The mud made it easier to track Skip and Max and all the horses they were taking with them. They were headed for town for sure, but they had a good head start.

At last the rain stopped, and moonlight broke through again, spreading its glow on the wet land and raging creek. Tommy was curled up in the rocks just off the wagon road and a mile east of the gate, shivering in the rain, rifle halfway under his coat. His left arm was dangling, racked with pain, and his ankle was hurting pretty bad. He had dragged himself there, hoping someone would come along.

Now he heard noise on the other side of the creek.

Max and Skip had been doing all right, Max feeling her body as he held her. He had bound her hands in front of her, hoping she would awaken and enjoy his friendly hands. Since they were in the middle of nowhere, he had even removed her gag.

But when Melina awakened, he was kissing her cheek. She screeched and clawed at him and fought to be free. As her fingernails cut his face, he snarled and slapped her hard. She screamed so loud, Max tried to choke her to silence her.

When Tommy heard his mother's cry, he got to his feet, moved through the brush and saw them on the north side of the creek. Max was shaking her furiously and slapping her face.

Tommy drew up his rifle and threw a shell in the chamber, but he couldn't get a shot at Max without hitting her. The roar of the creek made it hard to hear what they were saying. Melina was fighting with all her strength, and Max was trying to control his frightened, whirling horse and her at the same time.

Max was yelling, his face bleeding. "Darn it. Knock her out!"

Skip rode around with his pistol in hand, about to club her, when Tommy fired, hitting him in the chest. Startled by the shot, Skip half rose out of the saddle, gasped and yelled, twisted crazily, and fell down into the mud, sprawling lifeless on his back.

Startled, Melina stopped struggling long enough for Max

to slam his fist into her face, and he dug in his heels, heading away from the rifle, not knowing who was there. The other horses followed some distance, then fell back in the rain.

Tommy was frantic, but he couldn't cross the creek because it was too swollen for a boy with a broken arm. He would be swept away, but he started dragging himself along after them as he shoved another shell into the chamber.

"Mom!" he yelled, but no one could hear.

Melina was still struggling, but she was so dazed, she could hardly lift her arms. Max hit her again, and she collapsed against him. When he felt safe later on, he stopped long enough to gag her with a bandanna.

When Max and his mother were out of sight and he could no longer keep up, Tommy staggered to a halt in tears. He dropped to one knee in the mud, and he wiped at his eyes as rain ran from his hat brim.

He kept going, but with his left arm dangling, pain coming in searing flashes, his ankle hot and weak, he had to rest every few minutes.

Now he looked through the cottonwoods, and he got to his feet, gazing back in the moonlight to see three riders coming at a gallop on the north side of the creek, riding a distance from the rocks and brush. Tommy didn't know who they were, but he needed help. He took a chance and fired his rifle.

He saw them rein up and he joyfully recognized Jackson, Kansas, and Colby, but not the stranger.

"My God," Colby said. "It's the boy."

They forded the raging waters with great difficulty, and Colby was first across. He rode over to Tommy and swung down. He knelt by the boy, anxious.

"Tommy, are you all right?"

"I think my left arm is broken this time. That darned pinto rolled over on me and took off. And they got Mom. Max and Skip, I saw 'em. And I shot Skip, I think."

"You sure did."

"Is he dead?"

Colby put his hand on the boy's shoulder. "Yes."

"I couldn't help it. Skip was gonna hit her with his pistol. And Max was hitting Mom real hard."

"It's all right, Tommy. All you did was kill a snake."

With Tommy riding behind him, Colby headed east on the wagon road, Seth at his side, Kansas and Jackson following. When they passed the Ramsey gate, it was shortly before dawn.

*　*　*　*　*

Max had made it to town just before daylight. Melina was still bound and gagged, her hands now tied behind her back. She was conscious and squirming in his arms as he rode around behind the Silver Dollar. He dismounted, threw her over his shoulder, and went inside through the back door. As he entered the office, she was kicking frantically, and he tossed her down into a chair like a sack of flour.

Weary of her, he then turned to his uncle's safe. If only he had some dynamite, anything to open it. He tried the combination, but it was locked.

"What are you doing?"

Max turned, stunned to see a wild-looking man with a scar on the side of his forehead coming out of Purvis's private quarters in his britches and long underwear.

141

"Mickey, you scared the heck out of me." Max collapsed in a chair.

"That how you treat your women?"

"She's given me a heap of trouble, but I got to get her out of town. Taking her to Pine Ridge to get married."

Mickey snickered. "That's doing it the hard way. Who is she?"

Max filled him in on the story. "So they killed Purvis, and Skip, and probably all the others. But I'm going to have that ranch, you can bet on it."

Mickey poured himself a drink of Purvis's whiskey. "I remember Ramsey. He was one ruthless fellow. I saw him kill a man who was praying to live. Shot him right between the eyes."

"Yeah, he was no good. So, are you gonna help me?"

"Help you against Kansas Grange and Colby Dancer? Are you crazy?"

Max scowled. "You're afraid of them?"

Mickey sat down and stretched his legs as he sipped his whiskey. "I'm not afraid of any man alive. But I'm no fool."

"You help me, I'll cut you in on the ranch."

"Maybe I'll just take her for myself."

Max paused, looking at the man's half scalp and severe scars, but he was afraid to say that Melina wouldn't even look at him. He had to play this cool and stay alive.

"Look," Max said, "they could be here any time."

"You said there's only a handful."

"Yeah, that ole black smithy Jackson, and Colby Dancer, Kansas Grange. They'd all been wounded pretty bad, maybe even dead. And the rest are nothin' but cowhands."

"So why are you shaking in your boots?"

As the men talked, Melina listened, heart crazy, body aching from pain and cold. Her heavy coat gave her some warmth, but she felt rain in her boots and her feet were numb.

Her hands were tied behind her back, but the rope didn't feel that tight. She kept working it as the two men talked.

"In the first place," Max said, "this side of town, we'll have plenty of help, for a price. And the other side of the bridge? They won't do nothing but lock their doors."

CHAPTER SIXTEEN

Even as Mickey and Max talked, Colby, Seth, Kansas and Jackson were riding into the muddy street under a clear sky in first light. As they neared the Silver Dollar, Colby transferred the boy to Jackson's saddle.

"Take him to the barber."

Jackson nodded. "I'll be back."

"But I can help," Tommy said.

"Now, son," Colby said, "you don't want a crooked arm, do you? Go have it set. Then you can come back."

Tommy hesitated, but the authority in Colby's voice made him smile and nod his head. Jackson rode toward the bridge in the afternoon sun, and Tommy kept looking back.

"The saloon's closed up," Seth said. "Let's check out the gambling hall first. I see a light over there. Then the hotel. And we'll hit the Silver Dollar last."

Kansas was grim. "Time to clean out this den of inequity."

They dismounted in front of the Silver Dollar but walked over to the gambling hall, and inside, they saw roulette wheels and fancy tables but no customers under the hanging lamps. There were two dealers having a drink at the bar, but the place was otherwise empty.

Seth checked out the back room while the dealers stood watching nervously. "No one here."

Kansas looked up at the lamps, scowled and drew his sixgun. He fired until the lamps came down in a heap of broken glass, oil and flames spreading. The dealers ran out the back door, and the fire began to consume everything.

Outside, Seth turned to Kansas.

"Why did you do that?"

"Being a preacher for awhile, I reckon. Sometimes you got to wipe the slate clean. Burn out the demons. Start over."

At the hotel, they found a bleached blonde, older woman in a feathered wrapper who greeted them with a smile, showing a missing tooth. "Gentlemen."

"Purvis is dead," Kansas said. "And I'm going to burn this place down, so you'd better empty it."

"What? You can't do that!"

"Ring that gong, and I mean now."

"But why are you doing this?"

"This is a sinful place, ma'am. And it's the only way to get two-legged rats to move out. Now hit that gong."

She turned to the warning bell behind her and clanged it. Then Colby pulled a lamp off the wall and held it high, ready to smash it. A dozen women came hurrying down the stairs. Three men followed, carrying their gunbelts and boots.

"What's going on?" one asked.

"Anybody else up there?" Seth asked, sixgun in hand.

"They went out the back window," a woman said. "That was

the alarm that the law is here."

"Good," Colby said, "we're closing this place down."

After chasing everyone out, Kansas set fire to the place, and when the three men went back outside, the gambling hall was a raging inferno. They could see men heading for the corrals to saddle up, for it was obvious Dead Man's Creek was going fast. Women were gathered around a wagon being hitched.

Jackson was riding back across the bridge as six men hurried past him on foot, heading for the livery, and he joined Colby and his partners as they went to the Silver Dollar.

Three hard-looking men came from the shacks behind the saloon, looking at the burning hotel and gambling hall, and they stood with hands on their holsters, trying to make up their minds.

Jackson, Colby, and Seth faced them.

"Get out of town," Colby said. "This place is dead."

"Heck, why not?" one of the men asked.

The three of them headed for the corrals. Four women came running from the shacks to join them.

Colby shot the lock off the door of the saloon, kicking it open and shoving his way through the bat-wing doors.

Walking inside the saloon, Colby looked around, but the room was empty. "Seth, you check upstairs. Jackson you watch the door. Kansas, cover us. I'll check the office."

Seth went slowly up the stairway, sixgun in hand while Jackson watched the street. Colby moved toward the door to Purvis's office. He was worried. If Melina wasn't here, he might never find her.

As he kicked open the office door, a bullet whistled past his head. He rushed inside, only to find Max half dead on the floor with a knife in his chest. He was trying to lift his Colt once more, but it clumped down at his side.

Colby knelt quickly and jerked out the knife, blood spurting. "Where's Melina Ramsey?"

"Mickey. He stabbed me."

"Where'd he take her?"

"Pine Ridge, I think."

"Back in Slye, was he there?"

Max lay flat, eyes glazed. "All Keos."

"All Keos and Ramsey?"

"Yeah—"

"A woman was killed. Who shot her?"

Max rolled his head, squinting, trying to see Colby. "Mickey. Didn't want no witnesses."

Seth came into the room. "Everyone's gone."

"Get him out of here."

But when they tried to pick him up, Max coughed, kicked twice, and died, so they dragged him out the back door and over to his horse by a nearby shack. They draped him over the saddle and sent the horse off.

They went back into the saloon and knocked down the lamps and set it on fire. Hot flames shot up from the wood floor and danced in front of the huge mirror behind the bar.

Back in the street, they saw men and women leaving in wagons and on horseback, all taken by surprise and figuring it was time to get out after all with whatever possessions they could carry.

"They're goin' awful easy," Jackson said.

"They ain't fools," Seth told him, "and men on the run are downright superstitious. With Purvis gone, they know this place is dead, and their time is running out."

"Right now," Colby said, "we got to catch up with Melina. Jackson, can you look after Tommy?"

"You bet. But I'd rather go with you. How about Kansas staying? He's not in that good a shape."

Kansas tugged at his hat. "This is a family matter. Seth and Colby are my nephews. It was their sister and my niece that Mickey Keo shot dead."

Jackson relented in surprise. "All right."

Colby put his hand on Jackson's shoulder. "Somebody's got to get back to the ranch and make sure it stays intact. And look after Tommy."

Jackson agreed, and the three avengers obtained fresh horses from the livery. They were also flooded with food and blankets and possibles from the grateful townspeople.

Colby went in to the barber's back room to say goodbye to Tommy. The boy was resting on the table with his left arm in a splint and his ankle heavily bandaged. He tried to sit up, but Colby put his hand on his shoulder.

"Just stay put, son."

"I wish I was your son."

Colby's mouth went dry. "I'd be right proud if you were. You were plenty brave, fighting your way back with a broken arm. And trying to save your mother."

"I want to go with you."

"Now, son, you know you'd slow us down."

Tommy had tears in his eyes. "Bring her back, will you, Mr. Dancer?"

"I'll do my best."

Riding out of town with his brother, Colby turned in the saddle to look back. The south side of town had been evacuated, and had burned down to nothing but fireplace chimneys.

Dead Man's Creek was going to be reborn.

They passed the wagons and riders on their way to Indian Station, which was abandoned, and they headed for Pine Ridge to the east, high in the mountains.

*   *   *   *   *

Mickey Keo was leading Max's horse with Melina in the saddle, her hands tied to the pommel. Her dark hair was blowing in the wind, and he was having a good look at her.

If he married her, he could sell off all of her herd and the horses, and he'd have a fiery woman to wed. He was sick of having painted women wince at the sight of him. He wanted a wife who had no choice but to be with him, and sooner or later, she'd get used to how he looked. He smiled at the thought.

But Melina was thinking only of escape.

She had looked back to see the smoke rising over the mountains, and she wondered what had happened. She worried about Colby and her son, and she was terrified of a night on the trail with this ugly man.

He reined up and rode back to her. "It ain't far now."

"What isn't?"

"Where that old preacher lives."

"But we're a long way from Pine Ridge."

"We're going to Willow Creek. They just found gold there, and that's where the preacher is. I come through there on my way to Dead Man's Creek. We'll get there tomorrow sometime."

"Please, why don't you let me go? I'll pay you."

Mickey snickered. "Honey, I want you and your herd, and I'm

gonna have it all. Once we sell 'em, we're heading for California."

"But I will not marry you."

He pulled his hat down tight. "If you want your boy to live, you'll be begging to hitch up with me."

Terrified, she stopped arguing and started praying.

* * * * *

As night fell, Seth was still tracking them. "They turned south, toward that ridge over there. But if we don't have a moon—"

Kansas was grim. "We'll keep going just the same. I sure hate to think of that woman out here with Mickey."

Colby's heart was racked with pain. He knew what a vicious man this Mickey Keo had to be, especially now that he learned this killer had shot their sister on purpose. That revelation was painful to all three men.

"He must know where he's going," Seth said.

* * * * *

And Mickey knew exactly where he was headed. At nightfall, they reached an abandoned relay station along a singing creek, next to a canyon. He took care of the horses and dragged Melina over to the building, which was barely standing, but it had a fireplace in the single room with a stack of wood.

He built a blazing fire, and she wondered how he could believe no one was following. His arrogance and fearlessness terrified her, and she knew he would kill her without hesitation.

Mickey made coffee and heated up beans, and he fed her, but he would not free her hands, which were tied in front of her.

He smacked his lips.

"You must know they're coming for me," she said.

"Yeah, I know."

"What are you going to do?"

"Wait right here."

"They could be here any minute."

"Honey, I know that. But I can pick 'em off real easy, and they won't want to hurt you."

He downed his coffee and walked over to where she was sitting in a leather chair. She shivered as he reached down and played with her hair.

"As soon as I get rid of them, we're going to get acquainted. After all, we're gettin' hitched."

Then he grabbed a handful of hair, jerked her to her feet, and slammed his hard mouth onto hers. His kiss was brutal and horrifying, and she wanted to scream, but there was no one to hear.

"Please, let me go."

They heard a sound on the roof, and he let go of her, shoving her back so that she collapsed in the chair.

"What the heck?" he asked.

And now the blazing fire in the hearth was shooting out smoke. Large billowing clouds of smoke that enveloped them quickly, and Mickey started coughing. He pulled his sixgun and headed for the front window, frantically trying to pull it open, but it was stuck.

Melina was gasping for air as she managed to free her hands. While Mickey fought with the window, she bent down and picked up the iron frying pan.

Now the whole room was full of smoke, and they couldn't

breathe. Sixgun in hand, Mickey reached for the front door and jerked it open. As he ran out, Melina ran after him, swinging the frying pan, trying to hit him on the back of the head.

Instead, she hit his gun-hand with a loud crack, and he yelped as he dropped his sixgun. He spun and slammed his other fist into her face, knocking her over backwards.

Then he turned, about to bend over to retrieve his weapon, when he paused. A man was standing there in front of him in the moonlight, a big man with twin holsters and a scar on his left cheek. In his right hand was a Colt revolver, aimed arm's length at Mickey's face.

Gasping for air, eyes burning, Mickey kept squinting until the man came into focus. "Who the heck are you?"

"Colby Dancer."

Mickey straightened, working his shoulders. "You killed my brother Miles."

"It was a fair fight."

"So you say. I figure I'm going to slit your throat and let you bleed to death for the heck of it."

"You killed a woman down in Slye. When you and Ramsey and the Keos robbed the bank."

For a long moment, Mickey stared at him, as if thinking *so what*, then he grunted. "She got in the way."

"She was my sister."

Mickey's lips curled down at the corners. "Well, now, I hope you're not going to shoot. This darned woman broke my gun-hand. It ain't fair."

Colby moved slowly to his left to keep Melina out of the line of fire. "Hanging's too good for you."

"You gonna shoot me in cold blood then?"

"That's right."

Colby felt sweat trailing down his back, and his face was damp, but his mouth was so dry, it hurt. He was facing the man who had killed his sister, and he was ready to blast him away. Mickey was starting to fall apart. "Listen, Colby, if you don't shoot, I'll tell you anything."

"Who was at Slye?"

Mouth working, Mickey cleared his throat. "Well, Purvis and Skip and Max. Oh, yeah, Billy. And Ramsey. And me and Miles."

"There were twelve of you."

"Yeah, five of our cousins, that's all."

"What are their names?"

Mickey rattled them off as sweat trickled down his face, his brutality given way to cowardice, and he managed to give some locations where the Keos could be found.

Kansas and Seth had appeared from either side of the house and had not moved, but they were now afraid of what Colby was going to do.

"Colby," Seth said, moving forward. "Let him hang."

Colby still held his weapon ready to fire, his finger on the trigger. His heart screamed to kill Mickey and rid the world of this scum. He hesitated, his heart crazy in his chest.

Mickey was turning pale, his eyes wild, and finally Colby drew a deep breath. "All right, drop your gunbelt."

Kansas and Seth bound Mickey Keo while Colby knelt to lift Melina in his arms and carry her inside. She felt so light and lifeless, he was sick with worry. He remembered her kiss, the way it had spun his head. He never wanted her to feel pain again.

If he had not come to Dead Man's Creek, maybe she would not have suffered so much. He couldn't sleep, and watched her through the night.

But by daylight, she was awake, thanking them all profusely, and soon she was making coffee. She had washed her face, and although she still bore black bruises around her eyes, and her hands were shaking, she seemed to be all right.

It was decided that Kansas would see her back to Dead Man's Creek, while Seth and Colby took Mickey Keo to Deer Lodge, where he would be dealt with and likely transported back to New Mexico Territory.

As they swung into the saddle to ride, Melina came to stand near Colby's stirrup, and she gazed up at him with a painful smile that tugged at his heart as she rested her hand on his boot.

"Thank you, Colby. Please hurry back."

The Dancer brothers tipped their hats and rode off with the prisoner, while Melina hugged herself. Kansas came to stand at her side.

"What are you going to do about him, Mrs. Ramsey?"

"I don't know."

"He's hard as nails."

She nodded. "I know, but—"

"Women always think they can change a man."

"What would it take to change Colby Dancer?"

Kansas put his arm around her with a grin. "I'll let you figure that out."

Two weeks passed before Colby and Seth were on their way back from Deer Lodge.

When they reached the fork in the road just past the abandoned Indian Station, they both reined up in surprise. The sign pointing to Dead Man's Creek was gone, and in it's place was a larger, fancier sign: WELCOME TO DANCERVILLE.

"I'll be danged," Seth said with a grin.

Riding through the pass was strange because their hunger for vengeance had been locked up at Deer Lodge, and now it felt as if they were just returning home from a hard ride.

As they neared town, they could see that the ruins of the burned-out nest had been cleared away. A new building was under construction where the hotel had been. A hundred yards short of the bridge, there was another big sign: DANCERVILLE.

Jackson and Kansas were not the only ones to greet them in town. Merchants came out of their doors in a hurry.

"Now that you're back," Jackson said with a wide grin, "the folks want you to stay."

The barber nodded. "And the town is also working to get the stage to swing back to Indian Station. And that means the railroad will come this way. And Jackson's going to be our new town marshal."

Later, Seth and Colby were unsaddling in the barn when Kansas confronted Colby.

"Me and Seth, we're heading out to find those other five Keos, but you are not goin' with us. We'll be back in a year maybe to check on your first-born."

"You're loco."

Seth stepped forward. "You know, Colby, I figure Melina Ramsey's your last chance to get human."

"That's right," Kansas said. "And as soon as you pop the question, you come back to town and let us know. We'll wait, but I figure you won't be ridin' with us. Right now, you get on that horse and head out there."

Colby felt a chill. "Why don't the two of you come with me?"

"No," Kansas told him, "this is a job you got to do yourself."

Colby felt sheepish, but he had changed. Maybe it was that fall from the canyon, the feeling that he had been in God's hands, and maybe his sister's.

When Colby neared the ranch, he was covered in sweat, terrified of rejection.

Tommy came hobbling out of the house in the twilight, his arm still in a sling. The boy nearly fell off the porch as he ran to greet Colby at the corral. Hobbs was right behind him.

As Colby put his horse away, Tommy was dancing around him, talking about the new town and how the valley was so different. Colby was filled with joy and wanted to hug him. Tommy led the way up to the house, with Colby and Hobbs following.

Inside, they found a crackling fire in the hearth and fresh hot coffee on the table set between the leather chairs. Colby sat down with relief while Tommy chattered away, and Hobbs told them about the ranch and an upcoming drive.

When Melina entered the room, Colby knew it without turning to look. He could smell roses, and he slowly got to his feet, turning with hat in hand. She was wearing a green dress with lace at the throat and wrists, her black hair cascading about her shoulders. The sight of her made his heart sing.

"Colby Dancer," she said.

Colby lost all his resolve. This woman was too beautiful for any man, let alone a man hunter with little to his name. He hardly heard the conversation from then on, and he knelt to put more wood on the fire. Hobbs made an excuse to help a protesting Tommy to his room.

"Don't worry," Hobbs said as they reached the stairs, "we'll eavesdrop." And they crouched quietly on the steps.

Melina was resting in a leather chair. Colby was tongue tied, still on one knee and concentrating on the fire, poking at it, afraid to look at her.

"What are you going to do now, Colby?"

"Kansas and Seth and me, we're going after the other five Keos. They're waiting on me."

"Before you go, I want to tell you about myself, Colby, because I want no secrets between us. You were right. My mother was half-Cheyenne and died when I was born. My father, he had dropped out of civilization to marry her. He went back to being a newspaperman. And he brought me up himself. He never told anyone because he was afraid they would treat me wrong, the way they had treated her."

Colby swallowed hard, still afraid to look at her. He kept poking at the fire, sparks scattering.

"I never told anyone, not even Lou Ramsey, because I was afraid it would make a difference. Does it, Colby?"

"No."

"I'm so glad. You'll have a lot of work to do on this place. We'll find a way to get the gold down, and we'll—"

"I wasn't looking for a job."

"But you're down on your knee, aren't you?"

He turned, but before he could answer, she was down on one knee in front of him, her hands at his shoulders.

"Colby Dancer, I love you so much."

Falling apart, he grabbed her against him and kissed her hungrily. She threw her arms around him, and he held her tight, crushing her as she kissed him back. Breathless, they drew back from each other, his arms still around her.

"Colby, don't you want to marry me?"

Tears came to his eyes. "More than anything."

She began to cry, just as Tommy came running in with a squeal. The boy dropped down and squeezed into their embrace. Colby thought his heart would burst with joy, and now all three were sniffing back their tears. He could hardly wait to tell Kansas and Seth.

Hobbs sat down with exhaustion. "Well, I'm sure glad that's settled."

Colby hugged Tommy and leaned over to kiss Melina's parted lips. *God*, he thought, *what a woman*. And now, any patience he might have had was gone. All of a sudden, he was a man in a hurry, and he had to find a real preacher right soon.

ABOUT THE AUTHOR

Western novelist and screenwriter **Lee Martin** grew up on cattle ranches in Northern California. Martin began writing in the third grade and, later in life, wrote and sold 43 short stories before turning to novels with 23 now published. Martin is also a prolific writer of screenplays, mostly Westerns.

Martin's recent novels, *The Grant Conspiracy*, *The Last Wild Ride*, and *Fury at Cross Creek*, all received rave reviews from *True West Magazine* and were based on Martin's screenplays, as is *Fast Ride to Boot Hill*. *In Mysterious Ways*, Martin's new modern suspense Western, received great critical acclaim from *Kirkus Reviews* and *Midwest Book Reviews*. *Trail of the Fast Gun* is the first book of seven in The Darringer Brothers series, all of which have been reissued in paperback and ebook by Vaca Mountain Press, along with many of Martin's earlier novels.

Martin left the practice of law to write full-time, primarily concentrating on Western screenplays and novels, and often converting one to the other. Martin's screenplay for *Shadow on the Mesa*, starring Kevin Sorbo, Wes Brown, and Gail O'Grady, was based on Martin's novel of the same title (Five Star Publishing, 2014). The movie was the second-highest-rated and second-most-watched original movie in Hallmark Movie

Channel's history when it premiered in 2013. The film also won the prestigious Wrangler Award given by the National Cowboy & Heritage Museum in Oklahoma City for Best Original TV Western Movie.

Several of Martin's screenplays are currently under option by producers. Two of Martin's screenplays, *The Siege at Rhyker's Station*, filmed in the Fall of 2020, and *The Desperate Riders*, filmed in early 2021, will soon be available on DVD and the novels will follow. To learn more, visit Lee Martin Westerns on Facebook.

www.ingramcontent.com/pod-product-compliance
Lightning Source LLC
Chambersburg PA
CBHW031237260626
47169CB00007B/2346